"Look At Me,"

Navarrone demanded thickly. "You feel it as much as I do."

"Let me go," Erin whispered, refusing to meet his gaze.

"I don't think so. I think now's as good a time as any to find out exactly what's going on between us and just how deep it's running. Don't tell me you haven't been curious. God, I spent half the night thinking about how you'll taste."

"I slept like a baby," she tossed back.

He laughed softly. "Liar. You're as tempted as I am to discover what this is all about."

"I already know. You're a bully and I'm—"

"Maddening. You're driving me nuts."

"If it's an apology you're after, you have it. Now let me go." She tried to twist free, but he drew her all the closer to him.

Navarrone drew a long, tension-filled breath. "Slim, if you do much more of that, we may end up getting ourselves arrested."

Dear Reader,

I know you can't wait to get your hands on September's Silhouette Desire books! First, because September has the latest installment in Diana Palmer's MOST WANTED series—*The Case of the Missing Secretary.* And don't worry if you missed earlier books in the series; each story stands on its own.

Next, because September has Annette Broadrick, and the start of her new series, the SONS OF TEXAS. This month we have *Love Texas Style!* Look for *Courtship Texas Style!* in October and *Marriage Texas Style!* in November.

And, of course, there's this month's thrilling, sexy, wonderful *Man of the Month, Navarrone,* by Helen R. Myers. And September is completed with fabulous stories by Laura Leone, Jean Barrett and a talented newcomer I know you'll love, Mary Maxwell.

Don't miss any of these. I couldn't begin to pick a favorite—they're all so terrific—and I'll bet you couldn't, either.

All the best,

Lucia Macro
Senior Editor

HELEN R. MYERS

NAVARRONE

SILHOUETTE *Desire*®

Published by Silhouette Books New York

America's Publisher of Contemporary Romance

SILHOUETTE BOOKS
300 East 42nd St., New York, N.Y. 10017

NAVARRONE

ISBN: 0-373-05738-5

First Silhouette Books printing September 1992

Printed in the U.S.A.

HELEN R. MYERS

satisfies her preference for a reclusive life-style by living deep in the Piney Woods of East Texas with her husband, Robert, and—because they were there first—the various species of four-legged and winged creatures that wander throughout their ranch. To write has been her lifelong dream, and to bring a slightly different flavor to each book is an ongoing ambition.

For Dale L. McCann,
who dreams of the wilderness
and best understands there are few worthwhile paths
that are straight or simple.

And to Ed,
who deserves his own nine-hole forest—
even if he is a Gemini.

One

_____

The eighteen-wheeler was at least a mile ahead of him when Navarrone Santee saw its brake lights flare. Sunrise was minutes old and, except for the truck, he was alone on the seemingly endless stretch of New Mexico highway. He'd just turned off his own vehicle's headlights, now that opaque blackness had given way to shades of pink, lavender and tangerine. The piñon and juniper were once again distinguishable as scrub and no longer shrouded, lurking figures, as a few imaginative, night-traveling tourists occasionally insisted to anyone who would listen.

He'd driven this stretch of the interstate hundreds of times in his thirty-seven years and knew the topography of every mile so well that, when the truck slowed, it was relatively easy for him to gauge that the driver was heading for the cutoff to Azul. His own destination.

A new guy, he decided. The veterans were already aware that unless they were in dire need of fuel, had mechanical trouble or were desperate for Carmelita Vachez's syruplike coffee, Azul was a side trip to nowhere. People had to have a specific purpose for going to the sunbaked, dust-bowl community, otherwise they would be hard-pressed to tell it apart from dozens of other similarly nondescript towns spread across the state. He doubted that many of Azul's few hundred residents could explain why they stayed. But he knew. What kept the majority from packing up their modest belongings and leaving was that they were either too old, too poor or too simple to consider going elsewhere. The rest—and it gave him neither pride nor pleasure to have to include himself in that group—were even worse off. They actually clung to the idealistic opinion that they could change, no, improve things.

Fools, the lot of us, he concluded with a weary sigh.

Lately it seemed all he had in him was cynicism, and it looked as though the trend was going to continue. His drive north to interview Joe Pine in an Albuquerque jail had reaffirmed that.

Joe, a full-blooded Navaho and sometime-resident of the community, had been arrested in a bar up there after attempting to put a man's head through a rest-room door. Minor technicalities, such as the door being made of steel and the victim being an Anglo had apparently had little impact on Joe, who'd been bent on teaching the guy a lesson in patience. Once at the police station, however, he'd risen out of his drunken stupor long enough to vocalize his opinion about a legal system wherein Anglos could get away with shooting Native Americans in Azul, while in Albuquerque, Indians couldn't use public facilities without being harassed. An alert cop, overhearing the remark and remembering the incident that had been reported over the wires, had phoned the Azul station to pass on the information.

At last, Navarrone had told himself, at last he'd found someone who might shed some light on the death of old Fred Guy. Like Joe, Fred had been a drifter, and one night two months ago he'd apparently been mistaken for a wild horse—lately the targets of random shootings—and had been killed outside of town on privately leased government land. Navarrone's gut instincts about Joe had been so strong he'd crawled out of bed and driven to Albuquerque at two in the morning to interview him. It didn't matter that Fred's death had occurred outside of the Azul police department's jurisdiction, or that technically he had no business doing any investigative work on the case. It didn't matter that once he'd reached Albuquerque, the cops there could have refused to let him see Joe. It was simply what he had to do. He wouldn't have been able to live with himself if he hadn't followed through on the call. Fred might have been one of society's washouts, but he'd still been an acquaintance. More important, he'd been a human being; he deserved justice.

What Joe had to say, however, wasn't going to be worth buzzard droppings in a court of law. No one was going to take an alcoholic drifter's word that he'd been in the vicinity at the time of the shooting, nor would they believe he could identify the vehicle that had driven away from the area. But at least Joe had reaffirmed Navarrone's gut instincts about who'd been behind not only Fred's senseless death, but the cold-blooded killings of all those animals. And that was enough to give him back the anger he needed to keep searching, listening, waiting.

For now, though, his anger had to be repressed, and the price of doing that was costing him. With each passing day the burning sensations in the pit of his stomach were growing more pronounced. He didn't need a doctor to tell him he was on the road to giving himself an ulcer, but he also didn't see how it could be avoided. How did you shut off your mind? How did you teach yourself to stop caring?

Nevertheless, he could do something about the gnawing that accompanied the burning. As soon as he got to town, he planned to blanket his acidic stomach with a plate of ham, hash browns and eggs at Carmelita's café. Naturally, ingesting a pot of her killer coffee would offset part of the food's therapeutic effect, but since he'd only gotten two hours of sleep last night—and it had been a four-hour round-trip drive—he needed all the help he could get to stay awake the rest of the day.

Instead of taking the Azul exit as he'd been anticipating, the eighteen-wheeler pulled over to the shoulder of the road. Now what? The highway was too well marked for the driver to be lost. He could have mechanical trouble...or maybe he was simply beat. It was common knowledge that some long-distance truckers pushed themselves to their physical and mental limits. Wondering if this was one of them, Navarrone decreased his own speed to watch.

No sooner did the truck come to a halt than the passenger door swung open and a young man climbed down from the cab. Even from this distance the guy looked to be all legs, and the rest of him was about as substantial as the scrawny trunks on the scrub dotting either side of the sparse landscape. It was almost comical to see the way he fought the weight of his backpack. The thing dragged him to the ground as easily as an anchor slicing through water. But Navarrone's mirthless smile turned into a grunt of surprised approval when, once on the ground, the kid hoisted the pack over his undeveloped shoulders and, with a parting wave to the trucker, started walking toward Azul.

Probably some college kid on summer break, Navarrone judged, flicking on his turn signal as he considered the boy's fluid stride. It took someone that young to be oblivious if not indifferent to the potential hazards of traveling alone these days. Especially to ignore the danger of hitching rides with strangers, he added upon seeing the guy glance over his shoulder, do a smooth about-face and stretch out his thumb.

By then Navarrone was close enough to notice he'd made a few errors in his appraisal. First, the kid didn't have slicked-back hair, but a long braid, which now rested over his right shoulder. Second, the braid reached past his breast, well beyond the length most men wore theirs. Third, there probably wasn't enough there to fill a B cup, but that gentle swell was definitely a female breast. In other words, he concluded with equal parts of chagrin and annoyance, the hiker wasn't a dumb college boy on summer break at all; *she* was a dizzy female who clearly had less sense than God had given a grape.

Though she no doubt had already noticed the light bar with its twin beacons and siren on the Ramcharger's roof, Navarrone flipped on the rotating cherry lights. It gave his reigniting temper an outlet. Coming to a stop, he noticed he had to readjust another theory; she was a few years older than he'd initially guessed. She also had the kind of smile that, for a moment, made him forget everything except how much he hated sleeping alone.

Grimly depressing the electric lever to lower the passenger window, he watched her walk toward him. Her jeans were faded from countless washings and emphasized her willowy figure without looking intentionally snug. Her shirt was a green-and-yellow checkered flannel worn over a white T-shirt. At least she had the sense to dress for the nights, which even in June could be chilly.

She leaned down to peer at him through the lowered window, and her thick, dark brown braid swung back and forth with languid provocation. Navarrone told himself any red-blooded man who wasn't blind or on his deathbed would have been tempted to wrap it around his fingers and draw her closer—to see if it, if she, smelled half as good as she looked. But when he lifted his gaze and met her stunning green eyes, he decided that if it weren't imperative to keep his job, he would've also liked ten seconds to give her a teeth-rattling shake for added measure.

"Good morning!" she said, with a smile that made the sunrise about as effective as a fifteen-watt light bulb. "Would you mind—"

"Lady, were you born foolish or is this a recent condition?"

Her captivating eyes were naturally large, even before they widened with astonishment. *"Excuse me?"*

"If you're harboring some kind of death wish, would you do me a favor and repress it until you're out of my jurisdiction? As it is, I already have more problems than I can handle. The last thing I need is some aging flower child who thinks the best way to see the country and make meaningful friendships is via her outstretched thumb."

"Aging . . ." Her teeth came together with a snap and the growl that erupted along with her expulsion of breath surprised him as much as the temper flaring in her eyes. What earned her a margin of his grudging respect, however, was that as quickly as she lost control, she regained it. "I don't know what your problem is, Officer—"

"Chief."

He watched her left eyebrow arch—with speculation or surprise, he couldn't tell which. "For your information, *Chief,*" she began all over again with brittle politeness, "I wouldn't have stuck out my thumb if I hadn't already noticed this was a law-enforcement vehicle. And if that surly remark about 'meaningful friendships' was in reference to my having just climbed out of that truck, you might be interested to learn I was only in it because my rental car broke down midway between here and the airport in Albuquerque. That driver was the first person to come by, and he tried to help me fix the thing before offering me a ride. Furthermore—not that it's any of your business—I am not, nor have I ever been a 'flower child.' And last but not least, I hardly consider thirty-two over the hill!''

Her voice, even while shaking with indignation, was husky, richer than he'd expected. Her accent was undistinguishable, which made it unique for this area. It had no Western drawl or twang, no Southern lilt; and yet as precisely as she spoke, she didn't sound like someone from the North, either. She sounded like someone who's gone to the best schools, a thought that roused his curiosity as much as her face continued to captivate him.

Oddly enough, though, she wasn't what he would call photogenically beautiful; her nose was too sharp, her eyes were really too large and her mouth... Well, hell, he thought, dropping his gaze to her unpainted lips, anyone could see it was too full and wide for her slender, equally makeup-free face. Damned if he understood why he was experiencing yet another sexual tug. But even after acknowledging that he was indeed wondering how her mouth would feel under his, it took a conscious effort to stop.

"Climb in," he muttered under his breath.

"What a delightful invitation," she purred back. "But on second thought, no, thank you. I'd rather walk.''

This time Navarrone swore to himself. He didn't need this. It would serve her right if he drove off and left her to her own devices. Chances were she would be all right. Then again, what if she wasn't? He had enough burdening his mind without adding a guilty conscience to the heap. "Oh, for crying out loud..." he ground out before adding, "I'm sorry, okay?''

She gave him a styptic blink. "You call that an apology?"

Those animated eyebrows of hers were shades more intense than the darkest hues of her hair; she lifted one with such haughtiness that Navarrone was tempted to floor his accelerator and leave her to spit gravel and fight off whatever two-legged and belly-crawling snakes happened along. He relished the fantasy for a full ten seconds before admitting to himself that he would be more likely to drive his truck into Elephant Butte Reservoir than follow through with the idea.

"Look," he began again, trying to gather the remaining shreds of his patience. "I'm willing to admit I was out of line to come down on you that way. My only excuse is that it's been a long night, it's going to be an even longer day, and right now I'd give this badge for just one shot of caffeine. So if you'll just get in, I'll take you to a phone where you can call someone about your car, and then I'll go have my coffee. Can we do that?"

After a brief hesitation, she reached for the door handle. Disgruntled with himself for letting it matter so much whether she accepted or not, Navarrone pretended a need to check his left rearview mirror for possible traffic and tugged the brim of his hat an inch lower over his eyes.

By the time he allowed himself to turn back to her, she'd climbed into the Ramcharger and settled her knapsack on the floorboard between her legs. Legs, Navarrone thought, his mouth turning as dry as the land around them; things were going to be awkward enough without his imagination fixating on those endless long limbs.

"So where are you headed after you get your car repaired?" he forced himself to ask, while shutting off his overhead lights and pulling away from the shoulder.

"Azul. I live there—that is, as of today I do."

Navarrone shot her a quick, startled look.

"Don't look now," she chuckled, "but you're staring."

He was doing more than that, he was putting two and two together, and he had a feeling the sum total was going to leave him with lots of egg on his face. "Oh, brother," he groaned. She couldn't be . . .

"Ah, so the news has gotten around."

Her amused grin held a mischief that took years off the thirty-two she'd mentioned, but it still left him feeling like a class-A jerk. "Everyone in town has heard about Doc Hayes's granddaughter Erin moving back," he replied dryly, once again focusing on the road. "They haven't had much choice, since you're about the only subject your grandfather's been interested in discussing lately."

"I was afraid of that. I hope he hasn't been making too much of a nuisance of himself. Or at least not as much as he did during my last summer here, when we heard I'd been accepted to his old alma mater."

"Can't say I know about that. I wasn't around back then."

"No, you weren't. I definitely believe I'd have remembered you. After all, you make such a distinct impression."

Because her remark, as well as her tone, was gently teasing rather than condemnatory, Navarrone relaxed. The lady knew how to be a good sport. He approved, and also appreciated, that. "Would you believe I've always been shy around women?" he drawled.

"Sorry. I'm not sure your credibility will stretch that far. Where were you—back then, I mean?"

"In the marines."

Her answering nod was thoughtful. "That must be where you learned the fine art of diplomacy."

Beneath his mustache, Navarrone's mouth twitched as he fought the urge to grin. "This relationship isn't going to get off the ground if you keep making me pay for that little misunderstanding back there."

"Why, Chief," she shot back just as smoothly, "I didn't realize—a relationship! And there I was thinking that after this, our conversations would be limited to lectures about jaywalking or driving over twenty-five miles an hour within the city limits."

"Anyone ever tell you that you've got a smart mouth, Doc?"

"Now and then. But before I'm tempted to apologize, I always consider the source."

His chest shook from trying to contain his laughter. Whomever he'd pictured when he'd heard that Doc Wilford Hayes's granddaughter was leaving her Peace Corps post in Central America and returning to reestablish his old practice, that person wasn't the one seated beside him. She looked like the kind of woman who'd been the college homecoming queen, possessing a mixture of all-American freshness and a classy sexiness that was as undeniable as it was appealing.

"You don't strike me as the type to have spent the last four years roughing it in the toughest parts of Guatemala and Honduras," he said, giving in to his curiosity about her.

"Really? If you don't mind, I'll resist asking you for your definition of what that type would be. And actually, I never considered what I was doing as roughing it. In fact, most of the time I had some of the best accommodations available. Believe me, sleeping on a woven mat can make you feel guilty when you see almost everyone else making do with less."

Navarrone kept his eyes on the road, but the new wave of surprise and respect rising within him was considerable. Still, when he spoke, all he showed was wry skepticism. "Then you're going to feel right at home in Azul. The per-capita income is still barely two-thirds of the national average. How the devil you'll be able to afford to keep your practice supplied with the necessary medicines you'll need when most of your patients will offer to pay you with a goat, or hint for a freebie, is beyond me."

"My grandfather managed, and so will I."

"Dr. Hayes, with all due respect, your grandfather doesn't do much practicing these days, and though he's liked well enough, there are more than a few people who consider him to have a couple of screws loose. But at least he can attribute his eccentricities to age. What's your excuse?"

"Maybe I'm a young eccentric. Or maybe money has simply never been a great motivator for me."

That was not only commendable, it paralleled his own attitude toward life. But philosophizing was one thing; acting on those ideas was something else. "Fine. Just don't be surprised if people remain a little leery about your good intentions."

She was silent a moment and then quietly replied, "Do you know anything about my parents, Chief?"

"No, as a matter of fact, I don't. Wil doesn't talk about them, so I'd always assumed they'd passed away years ago."

"On the contrary. They're alive and well and living in Beverly Hills where my father does a thriving business performing cosmetic surgery on the already beautiful and affluent. I'm talking about people who are so bored their chief preoccupation is to medically remove as much of the history of their existence from their faces as possible. Periodically, even my father realizes he's not satisfying the objectives he'd set for himself when he took the Hippocratic oath, so to appease his disquiet he either wires me money to buy supplies or else he ships them directly to wherever I am. He's aware of what kind of economic environment this is. I have no doubt the arrangement will continue.''

Well, well, Navarrone thought, he really had underestimated her. The homecoming queen harbored some strong feelings along with all her spunk. He liked that, and despite their shaky start, he was feeling an increasingly strong attraction to her. That wasn't unwelcome news, either. It was about time something positive offset all the negatives in his life.

They were approaching downtown Azul, a half-dozen streets that from the sky—a sight he'd had the opportunity to view when he'd participated in a countywide search for a missing child—looked like a slightly twisted ticktacktoe board. A third of the streets were so badly potholed that the resulting lack of traffic had driven most of the stores there out of business. Kids now used those areas to play what they called ''suicide soccer.''

Most of the buildings in town were forty or more years old and adobe, which the sun and wind had bleached to where they now resembled a man-made mesa. The few wood structures in town appeared fragile and ready to tip over in the next windstorm. Most of the stores stood in groups of threes and fours, and many units had at least one shop empty. But not the first building on the left.

''Are you hungry?'' Navarrone asked.

''Is that an invitation?''

''Everyone in town knows Wil isn't expecting you until this afternoon, and he generally shows up at the café for breakfast. You might as well join me there and wait for him.''

Like many of the other stores, the café had no sign out front. Over the years Carmelita had frequently voiced her ire at having to carry it from location to location—after greedy landlords forced her to relocate through rental increases or refusing to do simple building maintenance—until she'd abandoned the sign entirely. Her current place of business had formerly been a funeral parlor. Navarrone smiled inwardly as he recalled her delight at inheriting its huge walk-in refrigerator.

Though she hadn't given him an answer, he took his passenger's silence as an affirmative reply and cut across Main Street to park diagonally in the open slot between two dusty and scarred pickup trucks. After shutting off the engine, he turned to face Erin and found her viewing the café with a nostalgic expression, further softening her feminine face.

"Sometimes I still dream about Carmelita's apple-spice pancakes," she said, her voice so low Navarrone wasn't sure whether her comment was directed at him or was more of a private reflection.

He couldn't take his eyes off her mouth. "Is this a roundabout way of telling me the way to your heart is through your stomach?"

For a moment he thought she might not have heard him, but then she gave him a slow, sidelong look. He couldn't quite identify the emotion darkening her eyes. Not for a moment would he have believed it was nervousness, not in a woman with her kind of confidence, yet that was his first impression.

"Not hardly," she murmured. "I'd better warn you, though—I have a big appetite."

He let his gaze slide over her slender torso. "I reckon I can afford you."

Something changed during the silence that followed. He felt it like a hair-trigger response and could tell by the slight parting of her lips that she did, too. Suddenly the flippancy underscoring their banter gave way to something less casual, something beyond flirtatiousness. Navarrone knew if he hadn't parked in clear view of the two old-timers unabashedly watching them from their regular table by the café's front window, he would have identified what taste lingered on those lips, learned if she kept her eyes open or shut during a kiss, discovered if she made any sounds when he deepened the caress and stroked his tongue against—

"Don't you think you should at least introduce yourself before you begin doing that to a woman?" she asked, her voice dropping to a cadence that could only be described as dark velvet.

"Doing what?"

"Undressing her with your eyes."

"Give me a little credit, Doctor. I hadn't gotten past your mouth. Yet."

Color crept into her cheeks, and just before she lowered her eyelashes—the kind that even on a woman seemed an unfair advantage—Navarrone saw a flash of something that had him wondering again. Then her eyes were hidden from him. She shook her head and released her seat belt.

"I'll have to remember never to indulge in mental skirmishes with you before breakfast," she told him. "It's too hard for my brain to keep up."

Without giving him a chance to respond, she jumped out of the truck. Just as well, he decided. As much as he'd enjoyed the opportunity to get his mind off his troubles, he knew it wasn't smart to continue allowing his impulses to override common sense. The lady definitely was having a strange effect on him. He couldn't remember the last time he'd flirted with a woman quite this way.

Bemused, he followed her to the front door of Carmelita's, but as she reached for the handle, he couldn't resist placing his left palm against the steel frame to keep it shut. Maybe he was right to question his reaction to her, but that didn't mean he was quite ready to share her with anyone else.

When she lifted her head and gave him another of those arched, querying looks, he extended his right hand and took her knapsack with his left. "The name's Santee. Navarrone Santee."

She stared at his hand for several seconds before giving him hers, and with a casualness he suspected was at least partially forced, said, "Yes, I know."

Though Erin had once considered herself to have a healthy sense of humor, it had been months since she'd felt more than a flickering of its existence. Even in happier days, though, she'd rarely been the type to play mind games. Yet from the moment she'd walked up to his truck, this big lawman had been triggering those responses in her. More disconcerting was the conscious and unconscious sexuality simmering beneath his words and glances. But at least she could take satisfaction in knowing that, despite her being out of practice, she seemed to be holding her own.

Truth be known, she'd been aware of who he was from the moment he'd corrected her about his proper title. That was the only reason she hadn't refused a ride.

Her grandfather had written about Azul's chief of police so often she felt she already knew him. Gramps had called him a crusader, proud but fair, hard as the land he protected and a dangerous man to cross.

But what her grandfather had failed to impart was that Navarrone Santee gave new meaning to the term *machismo*. She was beginning to suspect his negligence had been intentional, as if he'd known what kind of reaction they would spark in each other—and how hard she would work to resist it. She was going to have to straighten out the old fox on a few things as soon as possible. She could use a few chuckles in her life and she wasn't against a bit of flirting, provided it wasn't taken seriously. Navarrone Santee, however, didn't strike her as the kind of man to be satisfied with merely that, and she wasn't in any condition to deal with more.

As she watched admiration replace curiosity in warm, probing eyes, which were as black as his hair and mustache, she acknowledged he looked exactly the way Gramps had described him: long, lean and anything but dismissable. A no-nonsense five foot eight herself, he stood a good six inches taller. Ever since the episode in Honduras, men with his build had a tendency to intimidate her. Her professional eye gauged he would tip a scale at one hundred eighty-five pounds or so, and every inch of flesh beneath his blue Western shirt and jeans seemed to be honed muscle. Yes, she had reason to be sensitive to the contrasts between them. Still, she felt maybe not exactly safe—she doubted she would ever know such a luxury again—but confident that this was a man who kept his emotions in careful check. Nevertheless, she withdrew her hand as quickly as manners allowed.

They entered the restaurant. No sooner did Navarrone hang his hat than their presence created an uproar behind the counter. Carmelita, pausing midsentence in an argument with her cook, gave a shriek of recognition and thrust a spatula back into the hands of the battle-weary man. Then she raced from behind the half wall separating the kitchen from the dining area.

The middle-aged proprietor was a broad-shouldered, stout woman, the variety of earth mother whose jovial slap on the back could give a grown man whiplash and whose buxom breasts were ample for soothing two weepy children at once. Her lush hair had remained the same coal black Erin remembered, and she still wore it in a meticulous thick braid fastened around her head. But what delighted Erin most was once again witnessing how the woman's round cheeks squeezed her dark eyes into two merry slits, as she broke into a gap-toothed grin.

Her barrage of greetings was followed by recriminations to Navarrone because he hadn't called ahead to let her know they were on their way. "Men," she scoffed in Spanish. "Without a woman's direction, you're all lost." Whereupon she engulfed Erin in a suffocating hug. "Let me see you," she eventually demanded, switching to near-perfect English. Abruptly stepping back, she framed Erin's face with her broad, callused hands. "All grown and a doctor, just like your grandpapa. But so skinny." She clucked her tongue several times, before directing Erin and Navarrone to a booth. "No matter, we fix. Sit. I know exactly what you need."

It was dizzying, it was wonderful, and as she slid onto the black vinyl bench—where Navarrone had already set her backpack—Erin felt like a child again. "I'd forgotten how overwhelming she can be," she admitted wryly to the man who eased himself onto the opposite seat.

"I take it you used to come in here a lot when you visited Wil?"

"Uh-huh. I hadn't yet learned how to cook, and he wasn't much better, so it was either that or survive on canned goods. Back then she was still in—" Erin glanced out the café's front window "—well, down the street somewhere. I have to admit, though, things haven't changed all that much."

"Carmelita doesn't believe in altering what's proved to work for her," Navarrone drawled, as she continued her inspection.

Erin considered the industrious brown spider widening its web in the corner above his head and grinned. It was impossible, of course, but the arachnid bore a remarkable resemblance to the one she remembered residing at the other location.

A teenage girl Erin didn't recognize came over with mugs and a pot of fresh coffee. She filled the mugs and then laid out crisp cloth napkins and sparkling silverware, which she dug out of the deep pockets of her immaculate apron. That was the thing about Carmelita's café, Erin noted with a sigh of satisfaction; there could be cobwebs filling corners and fingerprints on the windows and doors, but whatever and whoever touched food had to be spotless.

"Feels good, doesn't it?"

Realizing he'd heard her sigh, Erin looked back at Navarrone. Once again she found herself ensnared by his dark gaze. She'd never seen eyes so confident and yet brooding. "Yes, it feels nostalgic…eerie…nice. I was still a child when I left Azul. Young and ready to save the world."

"From what I hear, you didn't do a half-bad job," he replied, pouring a few drops of cream into his coffee.

Erin was only too aware of where he'd obtained that bit of information, and she shot him a droll look. "In case you haven't already figured it out, Gramps is a charter member of braggarts anonymous. My accomplishments might read impressively on paper, but I was only one small part of a huge, overburdened and underbudgeted system. Still, I like to think I've done some good."

"Why did you quit?"

Memories, never too far away, came back with a nightmare's intensity, and for a moment Erin didn't see the strong-jawed lawman sitting before her, but other faces, more blunt featured and cruel. She shook her head, rejecting the vision and the memories. "It…it was time."

"Burnout?"

"Something like that." She picked up her coffee mug and concentrated on drinking the pungent brew. Carmelita's special blend was unforgettably bitter, but effective at clearing one's mind, which was exactly what she needed. "Tell me about you," she prompted, aware he was continuing to study her as though she were a variety of tough nut he'd acquired a taste for. "This is your what—second year as chief of police? Have you found it to be what you'd expected or wanted?"

"Being a cop is all I ever wanted to be. As for expectations, I learned to abandon those about twenty minutes after I took office."

Decisiveness and self-deprecating humor; the combination was as contradictory as his looks. He had naturally bronze skin, yet his face, long rather than narrow, was highlighted by a straight Anglo nose, squared chin and—beneath a sharp brow and low eyebrows that could represent any ethnicity—deep-set knowing eyes. "Your features are an interesting blend of nationalities, and so is your name," she said, studying him with clinical interest. "I can't decide whether you're Indian, Hispanic or—Scots, maybe?"

"Mexican on my mother's side and a little bit of everything on my father's, but most recently Welsh and Santee Sioux."

"Santee—of course. Your parents must be striking people."

"They were."

His voice, already a rich baritone, spoke volumes, and Erin felt a quick surge of compassion. "I'm sorry, I didn't know. What I meant was that you're very good-looking." Seeing the corners of his mouth lift and disappear under his neatly trimmed mustache, she shrugged. "Don't tell me you've never been told that before?"

He glanced over to the noisy group of people trudging in. "Never by an Anglo girl I'd just met ten minutes before."

"I'm a little old to be called a girl, Chief Santee. Furthermore, I was referring to your genetic bone structure, not your potential sex appeal."

"Well, now that the subject's been brought up, feel free."

Helpless to resist, Erin allowed a slow laugh. "Far be it from me to add to the delinquency of a peace officer." Intent on sparing her nerves another round of verbal dueling, she eased herself out of the booth. "If you'll excuse me for a moment, I'm going to go wash the dust off my hands before Carmelita brings us our food."

She crossed the wide dining area and headed toward the rest rooms. Just before she turned down the hall, she became aware of heavy footsteps, someone moving quickly behind her. Before she could glance over her shoulder, a strong arm snaked around her waist, a hand covered her eyes. In the next instant she was being lifted off her feet and drawn against a solid body. Shocked and horrified, she barely heard the drawled "Guess who?" of her attacker. Instead, memories of another time, another place, plunged her into a mindless terror. Panic chased a scream of denial up her throat, and functioning on pure reflex, she began to fight back with every ounce of strength she possessed.

It couldn't have lasted more than seconds, hardly long enough for her to understand her attacker's protests. As it was, she barely identified Navarrone's voice, a vicious growl spitting out, "Keegan!" Then she was free and falling.

Her shoulder hit the wall. Ignoring a spasm of pain, she swung around, because on another level she was already realizing she'd made a dreadful error. Worse, Navarrone— obviously thinking she needed help—had come to her aid, and he looked as though he was going to beat her assailant to a pulp.

"Wait!" she cried, just as he slammed the less powerfully built man against a paneled wall. She ran over to them and grabbed Navarrone's arm. "Don't. I made a mistake. *Please,*" she insisted when he still failed to release the other man.

Finally he did ease his hold. The young man used it as an opportunity to shrug off Navarrone's hands and grind out, "That's right, Santee, the lady made a mistake." But his expression changed into one of boyish glee when he turned to Erin. "Hey, Green Eyes, you almost shattered my knee-cap. Just for that, come here and give me a decent hello."

"Oh, Griff, you idiot," Erin groaned, letting him draw her into his arms.

"Lord, but it's good to see you. And look at you—you've come back prettier than ever. The least you could have done was pine away for me."

Erin ruffled his light brown hair before turning to Navarrone. "Griff and I have known each other forever. Do you mind if he joins us, so we can..." The rest of her words died on her lips as she met Navarrone's chilling stare. "What is it? What's wrong?"

Drawn by something that overrode all her instincts, she reached out to him, only to be rebuffed by his contemptuous stare and the backward step he took. She might as well have been contagious, she thought, stung even deeper as he shifted his attention back to Griff. "Tell your old man I just found out there was a witness the night Fred was killed," he said so softly Erin's scalp prickled. "A Silver Edge truck was seen leaving the site. It may not be enough to get a warrant for his arrest, but I won't stop until I can personally put one in the sheriff's hand. You tell him."

As Erin stared with disbelief, he retrieved his hat and strode out of the café.

Two

"Why that no-account, arrogant—"

"Griff, no!" As he began to follow Navarrone Santee, Erin grabbed Griffin Keegan's arm. She herself was upset with the policeman's behavior. However, a brawl in the street wasn't going to solve anything. "Let him go."

"He's been an irritation to me and my family for as long as I can remember. It's about time I put an end to it."

Erin could hardly believe what she was hearing; the scene was like something out of an old Western movie. What had Navarrone been talking about? Who was Fred? And why had he seemed to take such personal pleasure in threatening Griff's father? She thought about the contempt she'd seen in his eyes when she'd come to Griff's defense, and for a moment felt a dull ache in her chest. She hadn't deserved his antipathy. Whatever the problem, she certainly had nothing to do with it.

"Guess again," she countered, uncomfortably aware everyone in the place was still watching them and that some people looked very disappointed. In her? No, she had to be imagining things. "I don't want either one of you to end up being my patient, especially not on my first day back. Come sit down over here and talk to me. My goodness, I'll never understand the male affinity for fistfights."

That drew Griff's attention. Immediately his boyishly photogenic face relaxed. A genuine smile warmed his pale gray eyes and curved his well-formed mouth. "You're right." With a parting glance through the window at Navarrone, who was already whipping his truck out of its parking slot, he placed a proprietary hand at the small of Erin's back and escorted her to the booth.

The waitress followed, remaining silent as she collected Navarrone's coffee mug. After replacing it with a clean one, she filled it, earning Griff's effusive thanks for her attentive service. He'd always had impeccable manners, Erin thought, lifting her own mug to her lips. In fact, there wasn't much about him that she could see had changed. He still looked much like the sun- and fun-loving boy she'd known years ago. Of course, he was thirty-three now, but his hair remained thick and wavy, with no hint of gray dulling its subtle color. His finely molded teeth seemed ever ready to widen to an irreverent grin. Except for some faint lines around his eyes and above the bridge of his perfect nose, time had barely touched him. That is, until she looked more closely at his eyes. There was a bitterness in their depths she might have missed if she hadn't been so well acquainted with the boy he'd once been. Was it because of this problem with Navarrone Santee?

"Would you like to tell me what that was about?" she asked, speaking quietly to keep from sharing their conversation with eavesdroppers.

Griff grimaced. "You don't want to waste your time listening to something that doesn't amount to small change."

"You two were facing off as though you were ready to kill each other."

"I was merely trying to defend myself, not to mention the family name. Can I help it if that breed is blinded by a major chip on his shoulder?"

"Griff!"

"I'm sorry if I've offended you, but I call a spade a spade. He can't stand that his mother was once a house girl at the Silver Edge. As a result, we get the treatment you've just seen."

Erin didn't care for slurs against Navarrone Santee's or anyone's parentage, but for the sake of calming Griff she remained silent. Almost. "He may have a temper, but while I spoke to him, he didn't strike me as the kind of man who would succumb to reverse snobbery," she noted, the lawman's face vivid in her mind.

"Take it from someone who knows him. Santee's always making up some wild story about me or my father, just because of who we are. It's not that I don't understand—we're one of the most successful ranching outfits in the state. It's only natural to be on everybody's hit list. Still, everyone has their limits. My father might be able to stay philosophical about it, but Santee pushes me to the edge of my tolerance."

"I'm sure it's not easy," Erin replied, trying to take all that in. "On the other hand, what he said about—"

"Enough about him." Griff reached across the table and enclosed Erin's left hand within both of his. As quickly as it had come, all traces of temper were gone from his eyes and his voice, replaced by pure male admiration. "What I want to talk about is you. Do you have any idea of how glad

I was when I heard you were coming back? God, I've missed you."

"Impossible," Erin replied, keeping her own tone blithe. "During my last full summer here you were dating half the girls in your senior class. Rumor had it the rest were hoping you'd get around to asking them out. And as I remember it, nothing changed while I was away in college and medical school."

"Were you jealous?" he asked hopefully.

"Dear Griff. I'm afraid not. Losing my head over a boy— even if he was too cute for words—wasn't on my agenda."

"At least you thought I was cute," he said with a dramatic sigh.

The mournful response he gave her had Erin shaking her head. "Don't you play the dejected suitor with me, Griffin Keegan. We both know you've always enjoyed playing the field."

"Only because I was waiting for you to come to your senses."

"I did. Instead of becoming a rancher and building the second biggest herd to yours, I decided to become a doctor."

With a rueful laugh, Griff dropped his gaze to her ringless hand. "I don't think you realize what a challenge you are to a man."

"How's your father?" Erin said, redirecting the conversation to safer territory. "I understand he's had his share of misfortune."

Griff nodded. "He's confined to a wheelchair, but he's lucky to even be there. A few months ago, despite his heart condition, the old wrangler insisted on riding out to check on his new bull calves. A rabbit spooked his mount and threw him down a ravine. The fall itself should have killed him, but you know what a tough character he is. It did weaken him, though, and his doctor advised he'll either stay put in that chair or he can find himself a new specialist to drive to drink.''

Erin recalled something else her grandfather had written. "Any luck changing his mind about having surgery? The success ratio these days should make him feel more optimistic."

"Not to hear him tell it. He's adamant about not going under some 'sadist's knife,' as he puts it. But enough of that. It's hardly a worthy topic for your homecoming." He stroked his thumbs against her skin. The gesture was light and more affectionate than seductive. "Tell me about you. I want to hear all about your travels, the things you've seen...."

"Slow down," Erin said with a forced laugh, as their waitress came to refill their mugs. Undemanding though his touch had been, she was relieved for the opportunity to free her hand. "This hasn't been one long vacation junket I've been on. I was part of a team maintaining a rural hospital. When we did travel out of our village clinics, it was mostly to dense forests where we were usually overwhelmed with patients. There wasn't much time to notice the scenery."

Even as she realized she'd used the inclusive "we," Erin saw Griff's expression grow somber. "I heard about what happened to your fiancé," he said.

She nodded, hoping he would leave it at that, all the while knowing she wouldn't be so lucky.

"Wil says you were there when it happened. It must have been terrible."

Grief, still brutal and debilitating, stormed through Erin. She closed her eyes, steeling herself against it and the memories. "I'm not ready to talk about that, Griff. I know it's been almost eight months, but I can't. I'm sorry."

"Of course. I shouldn't have brought it up." He straightened in his seat and shot her a bright smile. "I have an ingenious idea. Let's talk about the future."

"A very wide and uncharted place," Erin replied drolly.

"Not if I have any say in the matter. Maybe you're not ready to hear this, but I want you to know I'm here for you no matter what. I don't care whether it's just to talk or you need someone to whisper sweet nothings in your ear. I'm your man, got it?"

Erin couldn't help smiling at his boldness and his charm. Though a year her senior, his off-the-cuff style and admittedly fickle behavior toward the majority of her sex had always made her feel older. "I see you're still painfully modest."

"I'm the best catch in this county and everyone knows it. Why waste time being falsely modest?"

She was about to comment on that when the front door opened again, and an elderly man with snow-white hair and a pink face shuffled in. "Gramps!" Erin bolted from her seat and hurried toward him, arms outstretched. "Oh, Gramps, how good to see you!"

Dr. Wilford Hayes paused and peered at her over the metal rims of his glasses before breaking into a wide grin. Then he rushed toward her, his speed belying his seventy-five years. He'd always been a slender, small-boned man not much taller than her, but now Erin found the term "fragile" a more accurate description than "wiry." His cheek felt baby soft against hers, and it was more mottled by freckles and age spots than when she'd last seen him. Still, he was a wonderful sight to behold, his features distinguished and his bearing dignified.

As he embraced her with his long bony arms, his laughter warmed her even more. "What a nice surprise! I thought you weren't supposed to get in until around noon?"

"I was able to catch an earlier flight." Erin briefly told him about what had happened with her rental car and how she'd eventually ended up here.

"Sounds as though you've already put in a full day." He glanced around the room, his intelligent but nonjudgmental gaze finally resting on Griff. "I suppose Navarrone decided he had pressing things to see to elsewhere?"

Erin couldn't resist a brief, derisive cough. "How did you guess?"

"Some things are a given, child. Santees and Keegans not mixing is one of them. Though we can talk about that later," he added, continuing for the booth. Then he raised his voice to offer a congenial, "Griffin. What brings you to town so early? I'd have thought you'd be at the ranch enjoying José's fine cooking."

As the two men shook hands, Griff replied, "I came to pick up some more of the Canadian bacon Carmelita smokes for us. Guess you know Dr. London told Dad that if he insists on feeding his heart pork, the least he can do is to make sure it's the leanest kind."

"Indeed I do, and I'll bet that's one of the few pieces of his advice Marsh has approved of. Can't say I've seen him giving up his cigars or whiskey yet." Wil eased himself in beside Erin.

"No, sir, he hasn't. It's not likely he will, either."

The young waitress approached again, this time carrying two heavily laden plates. She set one before Erin and then paused, looking anxiously from one man to the other.

Griff gestured to Wil. "You'd better take that, Doc. I need to get our order back to the house before my father gets downstairs and finds his own breakfast lacking its main ingredient."

"Don't mind if I do," Wil said, eagerly reaching for the plate. "Looks like Carmelita went all out with this, too."

"Guess I'll be going then," Griff said to Erin.

"I'm sorry you have to rush off."

"Glad to hear that, because I'm going to give you plenty of opportunity to make up for this. As a matter of fact, how'd you like to come to the house for dinner tomorrow night?"

"Oh, I..." Erin was momentarily thrown off balance. To add to her flustered state, she could feel her grandfather nudge her under the table with his knee. "Can I ask for a rain check?" she managed, recovering somewhat. "I've only just arrived, and you can imagine how much there is to do."

"Okay, okay, I get the message. I'll give you a few days to settle in. But in the meantime, don't let this old scrapper work you too hard, Green Eyes."

"Give your father my regards," Erin said, primarily to cover her grandfather's indelicate snort.

"You bet."

Griff bent to kiss her. There was no mistaking that he was aiming for her mouth, but at the last second Erin turned so his lips only grazed her cheek.

The café doors had barely shut behind him before Wil, slicing the edges off his ham, observed, "For such a small town, things sure do keep getting more and more interesting."

"Please. Don't you start with me, too."

"Wouldn't think of it—*Green Eyes.*"

Erin put down the fork she'd just picked up. "What a morning. What in the world is going on around here, Gramps?"

He glanced around the now-packed room and gave a brief shake of his head. "It'll hold until we get home. We don't want to insult Carmelita by letting this food get cold. Oops, here she comes now. Start shoveling it in, honey."

* * *

When he entered the police station, Navarrone ignored the snoring cop slumped at the radio desk. With newborn twins at home, Norm Weaver would be lucky to get any sleep there, and it didn't seem like anything earth-shattering was going on. He could catnap until Lou relieved him at eight. Besides, Navarrone wasn't in the mood to make small talk. He'd walked out of Carmelita's without his breakfast, and he'd go home and cook his own before he went back there today. At this point, getting chewed out by Carmelita would just about burn up what was left of his fuse.

To hell with Griffin Keegan, he thought, hanging his hat on the rack outside his office, and Erin Hayes could follow him there. He'd thought there might be something special about her, but he would be a fool to waste his time over any woman who called a Keegan a friend.

He stepped into his office and circled his desk, only to change his mind about sitting down. He was too wired to sit, and he certainly wasn't in any frame of mind to deal with paperwork. The smart thing to do would have been to go home and take a long shower—a cold one—he amended, remembering his physical response to Azul's new doctor. Not that he was about to give her all the credit; considering his nonexistent sex life of late, it was a small wonder he didn't take more of them. Then again, sex for its own sake had never been a high priority with him. He supposed he'd inherited that from his old man. Maybe.

His gaze was drawn to the photo on the credenza behind his desk, and he felt the ever-present sorrow he carried within him stir and deepen. The picture had been taken on his parents' wedding day, and it was one of the few photos in which his mother was smiling. Of course, in his family photographs were rarely taken, but the images he carried in his mind served him equally well. They reaffirmed that his mother's smiles had been like diamonds in a desert—rare. The Keegans were to blame for that, as well.

Drawing a deep breath, he stretched and flexed the muscles in his back. He didn't need to waste his anger; rather, he should put it to good use. Call the sheriff, he told himself, and pass on the conversation he'd had with Joe Pine. Kyle Langtry would find the information hardly worth getting excited over, but still, every item, every ounce of suspicion helped—and kept alive Navarrone's faith that one day he'd succeed in making something stick to Marsh Keegan. Someday...

But as he glanced at his watch, he realized it was too early for Kyle to be in his office. Exhaling in frustration, Navarrone went back into the main office to the coffeemaker, where he reached for the glass pot. It was then he noticed it was nearly empty, except for about an inch of sludge that made Carmelita's coffee look prime. Worse, the warmer light wasn't even on.

Thoroughly disgusted with the situation as much as he was with himself, Navarrone slammed the pot back on the warmer and grabbed his hat. He strode over to Norm and kicked his chair, almost causing the wiry young man to fall off.

"What's up? What's happened? Chief—hey, you back already?" Norm's baby-blue eyes, red from lack of sleep, were wide with surprise and confusion.

"No, I'm in Chicago. This is just an optical illusion. Make some coffee, will you?" Navarrone growled, tugging on his hat and heading for the door.

"What for? I mean if you're leaving and all..." Norm gulped as Navarrone stopped and shot him a glare over his shoulder. "I'll get to it right away, sir."

He felt like a bastard. Norm was a good kid and did a fine job pulling the graveyard shift, which no one else wanted.

He didn't deserve being on the receiving end of his foul temper. "Forget it. Go splash some cold water on your face before Lou comes in. I'm going home to wash up, myself. I'll be back within the hour."

The house and clinic was at the west edge of Azul, a long, narrow, cream-colored adobe structure trimmed in brown. The back half had two stories and served as the living-quarters section of the building. While in relatively better shape than most places in town, it was in dire need of a new coat of paint. A few flowers or shrubs wouldn't hurt, either, Erin thought as she and her grandfather approached on foot. There were no trees, and only a few native yuccas adorned the barren yard. Even the grass that had been planted years ago had given up any attempt to spread to the unmarked property boundaries. Sparse, neglected clumps were all that remained, and they, too, looked as though they would soon be succumbing to the fierce rays of the parching sun.

Nevertheless, Erin felt a strong wave of homecoming as they rounded her grandfather's ancient dust-caked station wagon. She paused, noting all the cardboard boxes stacked haphazardly in the back of the vehicle.

"Does this thing actually run, or do you just keep it to use as a storage closet?"

"Heck, yes, it runs. Probably has at least another five or six hundred miles left in it, too. As careful as I am, I figure I've got until next spring at the earliest before I need to think about trading it in for something else. Provided I don't get too many house calls," he amended.

His frown told Erin it was a technicality that had only now occurred to him, and she gave him the same unblinking look she gave her most recalcitrant patients. "Excuse me? You're seventy-five years old, Gramps. I don't think

I'm stepping out on a limb by predicting your house-call days are behind you. If there's any emergency traveling to do, I'll do it." She shot the green car with its fake wood trim a final, wholly skeptical glance. "And preferably in something Detroit manufactured in this century."

"Where's your environmental concern? This old girl might be showing her age a bit on the outside, but under that hood she's as fit as I am."

"I wouldn't invite any comments about your condition, either," Erin muttered, as she considered the fine veil of moisture dotting his flushed face. She reached around him to pluck out the handkerchief she knew he kept in his back pocket. Then she began gently blotting his skin. "In fact, when was the last time you checked your blood pressure?"

Her grandfather snatched back his property and glared at her from beneath the wide brim of his straw hat. "Yesterday, and it's no higher than it usually is when I walk that distance in this heat. And one more thing, young lady—I didn't agree to let you come back here just so you could boss or mother me. My understanding was that we were going to be partners in this venture."

As he wiped his face and muttered under his breath, Erin felt a stab of conscience. He was right; she had been assuming too much authority—at least, too quickly—but only because she loved him and wanted to be sure he would be around for a long time to come.

"We are partners," she assured him. "You're going to be my liaison and help me reacquaint myself with everyone around here, plus help me meet the newer residents."

"Hmph. Might have known. I'm going to be used for nothing more than an introduction."

"I'll also need you for consultations."

"Oh?" He perked up, reminding Erin of an alert terrier. "Well, that's more like it."

The sound of a rapidly approaching vehicle had them both glancing toward the road. Erin recognized the white truck right away, and noted that Navarrone Santee raced by without so much as giving them a glance.

"Hmm. You did rub him the wrong way," her grandfather murmured, sounding more intrigued than concerned. "He's usually friendlier than that."

"Never mind him." Erin linked her arm through her grandfather's and directed him toward the house.

They entered through the unlocked side door, and the scent of cinnamon and vanilla brought an immediate smile to Erin's lips. Letting a cup of water seasoned with those two ingredients steam on the stove was a trick her grandfather had learned years before from the grandmother Erin had never known. The resulting aroma was a natural air freshener, dispelling any mustiness or medicinal smells lingering in the shut-up house. It was also a clear giveaway as to how much Erin's arrival meant to the old man. Setting her backpack on the nearest dinette chair, she waited for him to hang his hat on the wall rack and then hugged him for the second time since her arrival.

"Well, now, what's that for?"

"I'm glad to be home. I didn't realize how much until I caught that wonderful smell and— Heck."

As her voice broke, the old man drew her back in his arms and patted her gently. "Now, now. If you start that, you're liable to get me going. Shoot, the sound of both of us belly-wailing is liable to send every critter between here and Socorro running for the hills."

His mildly irreverent humor helped Erin regain her slipping composure. "At the least," she agreed with a sniff.

Though she ducked her head and willed away the tears that threatened to spill over her lashes, she knew her grandfather's shrewd eyes were searching and analyzing; and as a result, the concern and regret that was soon reflected in their gray-green depths came as no surprise.

"I used to worry that the life you'd chosen would take all the softness out of you," he told her. "Now I think I should have worried about your not becoming tough enough."

"I'm okay, Gramps. Really. Just a bit tired from all the traveling between Central America and California, then here."

"Yeah, your parents wear me out pretty quick, too."

"Behave."

In reply, Wil gave her a stubborn toss of his head, which she ignored to pass on greetings from the son he'd never quite understood. When she was through, he continued watching her in the same uncanny fashion that reminded her she'd never been able to smoke-screen him on anything.

"So now we have that out of the way, tell me the truth about you. Are you still having those nightmares?"

Just the thought of them made Erin's hands go damp. She ran them up and down the back of her jeans. That was Gramps for you; he didn't beat around the bush, either. "Sometimes. Not as often as before."

"I'd hoped writing to me about the incident would have helped."

"Oh, Gramps, it did," she said, reaching out to him again. "You'll never know how much. It's just going to take time, I guess." She took a deep breath. "I remember how they warned us in med school about the emotional cost of losing a patient, but they never covered how to deal with it when it's someone you love."

Her grandfather studied her through narrowed eyes. "Erin. You're not blocking out the rest, are you?"

She couldn't quite bring herself to meet his probing gaze. "No, of course not, but . . . let's face it. I was the lucky one in all this. I have no right to wallow in self-pity."

Her grandfather shook his head. "That's not true. What's more, it's a denial. You have the right to feel raw, hurt and angry. Instead you focus on everyone else's needs and problems. Self-effacement is an admirable quality, child, but only to a point. Don't you see that, if you don't put yourself first for a while, take care of what's in here and here," he said, touching his head and heart, "eventually you'll be incapable of helping anyone else?"

"And I thought you said it was important to practice what you preach," she challenged, in a feeble attempt to lighten the tone of their conversation. But her grandfather's expression remained somber.

"I've taken a few blows in my time," he replied, nodding slowly. "I thought losing the love of my life when she was still a relatively young woman was about the dirtiest trick God could play on a man. Luckily I learned to focus on the good years He'd allowed your grandmother and I to have together. What you experienced, however, was a double blow, and no matter how hard you try, you're not going to be able to get past those memories until you deal with them head-on."

Erin exhaled, feeling the full weight of her physical and mental fatigue. She couldn't be more exhausted if she'd walked from Central America. "I hear you. Only I don't want to deal with them today, okay? I think what would do me more good right now would be to focus on the pleasure of being back. Being with you."

Her grandfather ducked his head and pretended to have discovered some stubborn breakfast crumbs on his crisp Western shirt and jeans. When he caught sight of her understanding smile, he gestured toward the hall that led to the rest of the house. "Well, don't stand there looking like you're waiting for a butler to appear and give you a tour. Make yourself at home."

Knowing she would cry like a baby if she didn't do something quick, Erin went to reacquaint herself with the rest of the house. At the doorway she crossed the hall and entered the living room.

Four years, she mused, wandering about the room, but little had changed. The green brocade couch, the sturdy armchair, the hurricane lamps—often used in place of electric ones—were exactly as she remembered, and so were the endless number of books and magazines piled everywhere in the same haphazard manner her grandfather had set them down. Erin smiled when she spotted a recent photo of herself on his equally cluttered rolltop desk. There were several more scattered throughout the cramped living room. She guessed she would find yet another upstairs in his bedroom, on his nightstand beside the one of her grandmother.

Her grandfather had moved to Azul from Albuquerque barely a year after the death of her grandmother Maureen. Erin didn't meet him until she was four, when her parents took a detour while flying back to California from a conference in Florida.

Even during that first meeting, something special had been triggered between grandfather and granddaughter—a recognition of spirits, a connection of minds. After two days, her parents had had enough of the New Mexico heat and barrenness and were listing excuses to leave. Erin begged to stay. She'd been too young, of course, so she'd been unceremoniously led off.

But when she was thirteen, she was finally given permission to board a plane by herself and spend two weeks here. The two weeks extended into a month and then the entire summer. It also started a yearly tradition that continued until she left for college.

Erin stopped by a table where she spotted a wood-and-pewter pipe rack and humidor. "This is lovely," she said, aware her grandfather was watching her from the doorway. "And old. Why don't I remember seeing it before?"

"Because it wasn't here back when you were. Navarrone gave it to me a couple of years ago, when he was going through some old trunks. He said it belonged to his father. Remembering I occasionally enjoyed a pipe in the evenings, he asked me if I would have a use for it."

At the mention of the lawman's name, Erin's stomach knotted with tension. Since the chief of police refused to be pushed to the back of her mind, she might as well use this opportunity to satisfy her curiosity about the irritating man. "I didn't realize you two were that well acquainted."

"I like to think we have an understanding. But Navarrone's not the type who seeks out the company of others. He walks to a different drumbeat, as the saying goes."

"I picked up that much myself," Erin said dryly.

"You saw him at a bad moment. There's no denying he's proud and has a temper. He's particularly sensitive when it comes to the Keegans. But as I think I mentioned in one of my letters, he's one of the most dedicated and principled men I've ever known."

"Is that a polite way of saying he always thinks he's right?"

"You're suggesting he's arrogant, and maybe he is on occasion, but I haven't come across too many men who have more of a right to be."

"My, my, you are a fan."

"I admire individualists, and he is one. He's also a tireless worker who demands a lot from people, but never as much as he demands from himself. We could use a few more like him around here."

Erin worded her next thought carefully. "Why haven't you ever mentioned the fact that he and the Keegans have a feud?"

"As much as I tried to keep you informed about the news in this area, I didn't think bringing that up was appropriate. Besides, it's been going on for so long... I guess like everyone else, I've come to think of it as just the way things are."

"Griff feels the conflict is based on jealousy, that Navarrone can't overcome his embarrassment because his mother once worked as a domestic at the Keegan ranch."

Her grandfather grunted with disdain. "The day Navarrone Santee sinks so low as to be ashamed of his lineage or how his parent made a living is the day I'll leave this place and go take that spare room your father periodically feels obliged to offer me."

"Then what is the problem between them?"

"Depends how deep you want to dig. On one level it's a matter of the law. We've been having a problem lately in the area. Someone's going around and shooting the wild horses that are running free on BLM land. Much of that government land is leased by ranchers concerned with maintaining an adequate supply of food and water for their stock. They see the horses as vagrants, trespassers useless for anything but dog food. Their lack of sympathy's started people speculating that it's one of them."

"How horrible."

"Or it could be some kids who've let things get out of hand," her grandfather continued. "Then again it might simply be a mean-spirited person out to make who-knows-what point. Human beings are a strange lot, as you know only too well."

"If it's federal land, why doesn't the government do something to protect the animals?"

"You're talking about a lot of territory, honey, and very little manpower or funding. The Bureau of Land Management is trying to help, though. Periodically they organize roundups where a bunch of the horses are herded and then adopted out to families or horse ranches—anyone who can prove they have the ways and means to provide proper care and give the animals a good home." He rubbed at the back of his neck. "But some individuals have grown impatient with the government for not moving fast enough on the situation, and someone's resorted to taking matters into their own hands."

Erin stared in mute horror. She believed killing of any kind spiritually decimated people, and her work and the experiences it had subjected her to had only intensified her belief in the preciousness of all life.

She wrapped her arms around her waist to fight the queasiness stirring in her stomach. "Navarrone Santee suspects the Keegans are involved."

"I know."

"But that's impossible! Griff wouldn't—"

"The last shooting occurred right on Keegan-leased BLM land. What's more, a man was killed in the process."

"Fred?" she murmured, raising her hand to her throat as she remembered the name she'd heard.

"Fred Guy. Navarrone knew him pretty well. Used to put him up at his place on nights when there was bad weather and Fred didn't have anywhere else to go. The day before he was shot, Fred had stopped by the police station to announce he'd gone a full month without a drink. Navarrone was mighty proud of him and was trying to help him mend fences with his family."

"I had no idea," Erin murmured, almost giving in to the temptation to sit because her legs suddenly felt unsteady.

Murder. She'd thought if there was one place that was relatively untouched by violence, it might be here. How naive she still was. And though she was pleased to hear Azul's police chief wasn't the bully his behavior with Griff had suggested, she couldn't accept that Griff or even his father would so blatantly disregard the law, let alone commit murder. When she said as much to her grandfather, he rubbed the back of his neck.

"I hope you're right. But just remember that you've been gone a long time, Erin. Remember, too, you were very young during those summers you spent here. Your days were filled with sunshine, freedom and dreams."

"What are you saying, Gramps?"

"Just don't jump to conclusions—*any* conclusions—until you've had a chance to observe things completely." When he noted her look of dejection, he was quick to apologize. "I didn't mean to depress you on your first day back. But since it looks like you walked right into the middle of it all, I guess you need to know what you're up against."

Erin lifted her eyebrows in query. "You make it sound as though I'm already torn between loyalties or something."

"If you stay, I think you could easily find yourself facing that problem."

She couldn't stop a brief, uncomfortable laugh. "I'm here to bring more medical care to the people in this area. Naturally I'm concerned with whatever is going on, but you know as well as I do that doctors can't get caught up in legal and political issues, which is what this really sounds like."

"You said the same thing in Honduras. Did it work? Did it protect you? Or Paul? Were you able to stay impartial?"

His questions were like physical blows, and Erin shut her eyes tightly against the ache that riddled her body. Yet even as she tried to block out his words, she recognized the problem she could be facing. She was a doctor committed to saving lives—all lives. Her work demanded she disregard all boundaries, whether they be racial, economic or political. On the other hand, life had taught her, in the most brutal way, that while there might be a dignity in that disregard, there was no safety. Not physical. Not emotional.

Her expression must have distressed her grandfather, because he crossed over to her and took her in his arms. "I shouldn't have said that to you," he murmured, stroking her hair.

"Why not? You're right."

"Being right doesn't interest me, Erin. Your well-being does. That's what I was trying to say."

"Gramps, all I did was spend a few minutes with an old childhood friend," she protested with a shaky laugh. "Let's not start blowing things out of proportion, okay?"

"Okay." Patting her shoulder, he headed toward the kitchen. "I'm going to get that disreputable excuse for a suitcase, after all, and play butler."

"I'm right behind you," Erin called after him.

But she didn't follow, not right away. Instead, she lingered a moment longer to glance back at Navarrone Santee's gift. She wished he weren't dominating her thoughts so. At the same time, she couldn't deny he was turning out to be an unexpected, yet central figure in her homecoming—a homecoming that was turning out to be nothing like what she'd expected.

Troubling situation. Troubling man.

"You get lost down there?" her grandfather called from the first landing.

"I hope not," she muttered under her breath. No, she decided, and hurried for the stairs.

Three

By the next morning Erin had done all the reminiscing and resting she could handle. Prior to coming to Azul, she'd visited with her parents, and she'd sat through a lifetime's worth of luncheons with her mother's friends, not to mention celebratory dinners, where she'd known even fewer people. Only the naps by the pool had been faintly enjoyable. Now, however, she was ready to return to reality. Her reality.

Used to long days, short nights and a high level of activity, she arose early and enjoyed her first mug of freshly brewed coffee as daylight delineated the San Mateo Mountains. After pouring herself a refill, she quietly made her way down the hall and let herself through the door connecting the living quarters with the clinic.

The scents changed distinctly, but Erin was very familiar with the sharp, rather metallic aroma of medicines and antiseptics. It had been within these dark paneled walls that she'd first experienced the stirrings of what would become an intense and unwavering fascination with the science and art of healing. From her grandfather's office, she went to each of the two examining rooms, almost hearing again his warm, caring voice as he'd told a tall tale to an anxious child about to get a smallpox vaccine; she smiled, remembering his dry humor when he'd convinced a hypochondriac that an appendix wasn't likely to grow back; and she could still picture the look of satisfaction on his face the time that stubborn therapy had helped a car-accident victim recuperate to near-perfect health.

There was so much history contained in these modest surroundings, and it had been achieved by such a dedicated, kindhearted man, that just standing there made Erin all the more confident that her decision to come back had been the right one.

His advanced age was forcing her grandfather to limit his practice to only a few hours a week. Azul was a small town, but there were enough people in the surrounding area to require a full-time doctor; as a result, he'd been finding it necessary to redirect cases elsewhere. That included anyone requiring even minor outpatient surgery.

Come Monday things would change considerably, Erin thought as she turned out the light in the second examination room. She couldn't wait.

A noise stopped her in the doorway. Before she could tell herself she'd been imagining things, she heard another sound—a door opening. Her first thought was that her grandfather was coming to look for her. But she quickly identified the sounds as coming from the front of the building, not the back.

Though she reminded herself that no burglar would have a key, Erin's heartbeat accelerated. Debating whether to duck into a room and wait or face the intruder head-on, she heard a female voice softly humming a soulful country-and-western ballad. Tension turned into bemusement as Erin rounded the corner and stepped into the reception room, her athletic shoes muffling her footsteps.

Some burglar, she thought, eyeing the young woman who was dragging in an old-fashioned, two-wheeled shopping cart loaded with cleaning paraphernalia. One glance at her shiny-clean but weary face told Erin that although her intruder looked as though she bore the burdens of the world on her shoulders, she probably wasn't much older than twenty-five.

"Good morning," Erin murmured, advancing another step.

The woman jumped and clutched the sweater she'd just removed to her chest. Its threadbare condition matched that of her loose blouse and slacks. Still, she was a quietly pretty woman. Her eyes were her best feature and were the same deep brown Erin had often seen during her travels through Latin countries. Their expression mirrored the nervousness she'd felt only moments ago.

"I guess we startled each other," Erin said, offering a reassuring smile. "I'm Erin Hayes."

"Oh, of course. Now I recognize you from your pictures." With an embarrassed laugh, the young woman smoothed a hand over her medium-length black hair, held in place by a triangular scarf of white eyelet. "I'm Teresa Aguilar. I clean for the doctor. The other—your grandfather." She reached into her sweater pocket. "I have a key."

Erin waved it away with a smile. "You don't have to explain. I remember now that Gramps said he had someone who came by." Then she added more somberly, "But with the clinic having such restricted hours, that doesn't leave you with much of a job, does it?"

"Anything is better than nothing, Dr. Hayes. I also clean store windows in town. And Mama and I sew for a dress company in Albuquerque. It keeps us and my two babies fed and clothed."

"What does your husband do?" Erin asked, having noticed the thin gold band Teresa was wearing on her ring finger.

The faint smile that had been hovering around the young woman's mouth wobbled and died. "Tonio was killed shortly after our youngest child was born. He'd been a ranch hand at the Silver Edge . . . but there was an accident with a tractor."

"I'm so sorry. I know how painful that must have been for you and your children." Seeing Teresa's skepticism, Erin added, "I lost my fiancé this past year."

"I didn't know. Please accept my condolences," Teresa said with a new warmth. "And, yes, as you said, it's been hard. Mr. Keegan paid for the funeral, but there were no other benefits in Tonio's type of work. Still, we have been luckier than some, considering the lack of opportunities around here."

"What if you moved to the city? Would that be feasible? Not that I'm trying to get rid of you, by any means," Erin added hastily, noting the young woman's stiffening. "I'm only concerned that, between handling all those jobs and caring for your children, you'll collapse from exhaustion one of these days."

"I'm strong, Doctor. Besides, Azul is my mother's home. She moved once for my father's sake, but she won't do it again. All my brothers and sisters live here, and her parents are buried here."

Erin was tempted to ask how many there were in her family, but decided against it. She had a feeling she already knew the answer: too many. Variations of the same stories evolved no matter where her work had taken her over the years. And it was so sad, she thought, watching the almost worshipful attention Teresa paid to the reception desk as she began to clean. First the young woman conscientiously turned the calendar to the proper date, even though the clinic wouldn't be opened today, then she wiped down everything from the phone to the ancient typewriter, including the stapler.

"Teresa," Erin murmured, beginning to understand what she was witnessing, "do you have any office skills?"

"Yes, Doctor. In high school I took all the business classes and graduated with honors. My teacher even recommended me for a job with an employment agency in Santa Fe. In time I could have worked my way up to being a counselor. But by then I'd met Tonio. His work was here, so I stayed. There are few office jobs in Azul."

"I know of one," Erin murmured half to herself. "Teresa . . . I think you're fired."

The young woman gasped in dismay. "But you can't!"

"How else will you be able to accept the job as my . . . personal assistant?"

"Me?" Briefly closing her eyes, Teresa whispered what Erin suspected was a prayer to the patron saint of struggling mothers. Then she burst into a shaky laugh. "I don't know what to say."

"Yes, I hope. You can't imagine how I worried about finding anyone who could type. Even if I thought I'd have time to do the work myself, typing is one skill at which I'm completely inept." It was a minor fib. She would worry more about how she was going to pay Teresa's salary. But manage she would.

"Yes. A thousand times, yes!"

"Good," Erin replied, feeling confident she'd made a sound decision. "Now all we have to do is work out the details. Why don't we go into the kitchen? I don't know about you, but I could use another cup of coffee.''

They had been talking for almost twenty minutes when Wil finally came downstairs. Erin saw that he immediately picked up on what was going on, and before long he began offering a few suggestions of his own. After Teresa returned to the clinic, insisting she wanted to complete her cleaning so she could begin familiarizing herself with her desk, Wil suggested he and Erin make their way to Carmelita's for breakfast. The phone rang before Erin could agree.

It was Griff. He explained that his father had experienced a restless night and asked if she would come out to the ranch to check on him.

''Griff, I can't do that. He's not my patient,'' she replied, apologetic but firm. ''No doctor interferes with another physician's case.''

''You won't be interfering. I just got a confession out of Dad. He followed through on his threat and fired London.''

''Well, phone his hospital in Albuquerque and have them recommend someone else.''

''That'll take time. What do I do now? He's really being a bear this morning. Couldn't you come out and look at him? I don't like his color, either, and he's coughing more than usual. It would mean a lot to me, Erin.''

With an inward sigh, she eyed her clean but worn jeans and khaki shirt. Hardly appropriate attire if one was concerned with making a good impression; on the other hand, if Marsh Keegan's condition was as serious as Griff suggested, changing would be a waste of valuable time. ''All right. I'm on my way.''

Erin explained things to her grandfather and suggested he go on to breakfast without her. After she collected her medical bag, which they'd picked up from the trunk of her rental car yesterday afternoon, along with her other things, coaxing the old station wagon's engine to start took more precious moments. But finally she was off.

The Silver Edge was almost a dozen miles out of town, closer to the mountains. Its name was a testament to the silver mines the state was known for. Erin passed few houses along the way, no great surprise since the general population in the area was fewer than twenty-five people per square mile. Those houses she did notice were way off the dirt road and almost as primitive as the land on which they stood. After having spent so long in the tropics, she experienced a renewed awe over the geographic starkness, aridness and almost brutal landscape stretching before her. In its own way it was breathtakingly beautiful, too.

The beginning of Keegan land was marked by a stone corner post, and thereafter recognizable by the miles of well-tended barbed-wire fencing. The turnoff to the homestead itself was at another stone-and-cement structure. This one included a metal gateway from which hung a sign adorned with numerous silver dollars. So it was still here, she thought with a wry smile. As poor as some of the people were, no one had ever been foolish enough to steal the thing. Erin had had to meet some of the ranch hands—as well as the patriarch himself—only once to understand why.

The house came into view, a two-story adobe structure with stone pillars spaced at intervals along the front porch. As she pulled up to the front, Griffin came loping out of the house and down the steps. This morning he wore a white Western dress shirt adorned with a string tie secured by a silver-and-turquoise slide. His dress slacks were a shade of gray that perfectly matched his boots. Here was a rancher prepared to wrestle a boardroom full of businessmen rather than a herd of stubborn cattle, she mused.

"You made it!" He barely gave her a chance to get out of the car before hugging her. "I'm really grateful you came."

"Has your father's condition grown worse since we spoke?" Erin asked, trying not to focus on the wave of suffocation she suddenly experienced. When, she wondered, when would she learn to stop freezing just because a man—even a friend like Griff—showed some affection for her? She eased back under the pretense of trying to see his face.

"No. But it's good to know you're close just in case."

A nagging inner voice had Erin questioning the real reason behind the call. As a boy, Griff had been known to pull his share of pranks, but she wouldn't be amused if he'd used his father as a ploy to get her here. She had serious work to do at the clinic; she didn't have time for games. Just as quickly, however, she chastised herself. Surely Griff knew it would be an exercise in extreme bad taste to pull something like that.

"Let me get my bag and then you can take me to him," she said, not quite succeeding at keeping all trace of doubtfulness out of her voice.

It had been years since she'd been inside the ranch house. Back then, she would come here when taking a break from studying or following her grandfather around—normally because Gramps ordered her to get out and spend more time with people her own age; Griff's invitations to go horseback riding had always been her first preference. Her impression of the house then had been that it was masculine and elegant but intimidating. Each high-ceilinged room had been dramatic, decorated with paintings of famous military battles and prized bulls. The furnishings had been equally austere. As she crossed the foyer, she wasn't surprised to find that everything seemed less intimidating than she remembered—but just as austere.

Griffin directed her to his father's study, knocking politely, despite both solid oak doors being wide open. The two men inside—one standing, the other in a wheelchair—immediately stopped conversing, and Marsh Keegan beckoned them forward with his unlit cigar. "I don't like what I see in your hand, young lady, but come on in."

In his prime, the patriarch had been a striking man; a full-length portrait of him hung on the wall over the fireplace testifying to the fact. He'd been tall, and his shock of chestnut-brown hair—now a coarser silver—had been as much a trademark as the winged brows over his fierce gray eyes. But as he broke into a hacking smoker's cough, Erin knew that these days he had to rely heavily on his money and political contacts to do most of his coercing. His debilitating and progressing illness had made him a shadow of his former self.

There was, however, adequate fight left in him to drill her with a gaze that was as unapologetically hard as it was direct. Though Erin could feel a professional compassion for his condition, she also wondered—as she used to—if the man had ever been capable of exhibiting any softer human emotions.

"When my boy told me he'd invited you over, it suited me fine, since I wanted to see how the skinny filly I'd known had filled out. Especially now that you've got him babbling like a hen-crazed rooster," he declared, his baritone voice still authoritative, if slightly raspy. His gaze fell once again to her bag. "But I should have known it was too early for a mere social call. Breakfast, hell, Griff."

"It needn't be more than that, Mr. Keegan." Placing the black leather case on the nearest armchair, Erin crossed to him and extended her hand. "Griff was concerned about you, and I can see why. But I've already told him you need a specialist—and to throw away those things," she added, nodding at his cigar. "It will suit me fine to say hello and be on my way again."

"Is that so?" The old man's expression gave away little, but his handshake proved as gauging as his narrowed eyes. "Haven't you become the diplomat. Well, considering what you've got planned for yourself with that clinic, I'll bet you could use a solvent customer. Are you sure you aren't tempted to assault me with that cold stethoscope I know you've got somewhere, just to write a hefty bill for services rendered?"

"Cold-stethoscope assaults are free," Erin drawled, patterning her sardonic smile after his.

"Free—hmph. You're Wil's blood, all right. Neither one of you've got a nickel's worth of business sense between you."

"Now, Dad . . ." Griff began, his smile brittle.

Erin signaled to him to let the comment pass. "Are you going to pick on me because you're nervous about being examined by a woman, Mr. Keegan, or is this lack of hospitality to hide that you caught a chill last night and really aren't feeling well?"

The shifting of Marsh Keegan's eyebrows was the only hint that Erin had scored a point. After a slight pause, he shot a quick glance at the man beside him. "I do believe I may have underestimated the lady, Van."

"It would look that way, sir."

After a low laugh that ended in a coughing seizure, Marsh Keegan turned back to Erin. "This is my foreman, Van Caulfield. He joined us shortly after you went off to play Livingstone or Schweitzer or whomever. Van, meet Dr. Erin Hayes, Azul's latest hope to join the twentieth century."

Erin's nod to the rough-looking foreman was polite but brief. It wasn't her intention to be rude, but she didn't care for the sly manner with which the wheat-blond-haired man answered Marsh any more than she cared for the insolent way he gave her a thorough head-to-toe inspection.

Apparently Griff wasn't thrilled with either man's behavior. He stepped up beside Erin and placed his arm around her shoulders. "Dad, you promised you would behave."

"Hell, this is as polite as I get and you know it, boy. Relax. I'm just indulging myself a bit, that's all. Damned little else I can do in my condition, isn't that right, Doctor?"

"The last man who tried to blame his bad disposition on his health had the opportunity to get intimately acquainted with one of my hypodermic needles, Mr. Keegan."

He slapped his thigh. "Atta girl. Don't take any crap from me. Too many people do these days. Pull up a chair. Van, you're set for the day, right?"

"Sure thing, boss. I'll get to that matter we were speaking of and..."

The rest of his words were drowned out by the sounds of a commotion in the foyer. Everyone turned to see Navarrone Santee standing in the study doorway, shrugging off the restraining hand of someone Erin deduced was probably the Keegan's houseman. One look at the lawman's face told her something was terribly wrong, but the prickle of tension tightening her scalp felt more like an electric shock when he met her bewildered gaze and she was awarded the full impact of his anger. Fortunately it only lasted seconds before he switched his attention to the owner of the Silver Edge.

"Call off your guard dog, Keegan, unless you want to sweep what'll be left of him off the floor."

Marsh grunted—whether in amusement or disdain, Erin couldn't tell—and waved away the stocky Hispanic. "It appears all roads lead to my threshold this morning. What prompts you to overcome your usual disgust with us, Navarrone? Were you concerned that Griff wouldn't pass on your message to me, or did you hope your latest accusation had finally finished me off?''

"You know better than that,'' Navarrone replied, his tone dripping with equal sarcasm. "I want you alive and kicking—at least long enough so you can face a jury and receive the prison term you deserve.''

"For my multitudinous sins, eh? Well, what crime have I allegedly committed this time?''

"Hired scum. A formal complaint's been filed against two of your hands. They arrived early this morning after a night in Albuquerque, not quite sober enough to eat breakfast in polite company. If you want them back, have someone stop by Carmelita's café and pay her for the damage they caused. Then have him come over to the jail and pay your men's fines.''

Marsh Keegan steepled his fingers. Only the shifting of his cigar between his teeth hinted at any internal agitation. "Anything else?''

"Yeah. You can tell them if they want to stay in this town they'd better straighten up their act. They won't be warned again.''

Van Caulfield stepped forward, but his employer gripped his arm. "My lawyer will be interested to know why the boys didn't get to make a phone call before they were incarcerated,'' the older man drawled. "He might persuade me to believe there may have been an infringement of their legal rights.''

Navarrone's bitter smile never reached his eyes. "Since when have you shown an affinity for the law?''

As he began to leave, he once again met Erin's stare, eyed the placement of Griff's arm, then glanced back at her. The look lasted only long enough for her to see that his opinion of her—already low—had just dropped several more notches.

Even before the front door slammed behind him, Griff was declaring his intention to teach him a lesson, but his father sharply vetoed the idea. The coughing fit that followed nudged Erin out of her own state, and she hurried to the failing rancher's side.

"Mr. Keegan, you're really pushing your luck."

"I am acutely aware of that," he rasped between coughs.

"Then if you'll allow a suggestion, the best place for you right now is upstairs in your own bed. Once you're settled, I can—"

"Thank you," he interjected, staring at the doorway through which Navarrone had exited. "But I'm afraid what's ailing me no one—particularly you with your little black bag—can fix."

By the time his truck kicked up the last cloud of Silver Edge dust and Navarrone was once again on the harder-packed dirt road leading to town, he had most of his anger back under control. Though the Keegans were by principle and deed his ongoing enemies, he normally had better success harnessing his personal dislike for them. The fire burning in his belly, however, was worse than usual, and he didn't have to think hard to figure out the cause.

Why the devil had *she* been there? he asked himself for the second time since spotting the station wagon parked out front. Hadn't anything she'd heard yesterday during that exchange made an impression on her? At the least she should have questioned Wil. Her grandfather stayed fairly neutral when it came to politics, but even he'd made it clear he didn't have a great deal of respect for the manner in which the Keegans operated.

Well, there went the idea he'd awakened with, to give her the benefit of the doubt. The woman had clearly made her choice. Why should he eat himself up about it?

Because maybe she didn't realize who and what she was aligning herself with.

Right. She was a doctor who'd traveled to some of the roughest corners of the world, not someone who'd just come out of a cloistered nunnery.

Caught up in putting himself through a mental wringer, he didn't notice for several moments that he was being followed. He gripped the steering wheel more firmly and peered into his rearview mirror. The density of the dust cloud behind him made it impossible to tell who it was, so he unsnapped his holster. There was, he reminded himself, no such thing as being too prepared.

The car got closer. It was a car, he realized with some relief, and not a truck. First he identified the vehicle's front end, then the luggage rack that told him it was Wil's old station wagon.

Before he could decide whether to laugh or swear, she signaled him with a blast of her horn. If she had put two fingers in her mouth and whistled, his reaction would have been the same—stubbornly he ignored her. When she hit her horn a second time and added a flash of her high beams, he gritted his teeth in growing agitation. She'd better have her windows shut if she didn't want to swallow the rest of the New Mexico dirt he was about to dish up for her, he thought with grim pleasure.

It didn't cross his mind that she would try to overtake him. In the first place, he didn't believe Wil's ancient wreck had enough horsepower left. But suddenly she was inching ahead of him—and steering into his path.

Navarrone hit his brakes. Like a hippo on ice, the Ramcharger's rear end slid back and forth over the dry packed earth, until it came to an undignified and bumpy halt. For all he knew the station wagon kept on going, but as the red cloud began to settle, he saw the vehicle idling only a few dozen yards ahead of him. "And that's your second mistake," he muttered, reaching for his door handle.

"Are you out of your mind!" he roared, as she scrambled out of her own vehicle.

"Are you out of yours?"

"You could have killed us both."

"You could have stopped sooner. Didn't you hear my horn?"

"I heard. I just didn't see any reason to pay attention."

"Why am I not surprised? I'm beginning to think you're one of those people who never pay attention to anything except your own interests."

The heat stirring around them was no more blistering than Navarrone's anger. He glared at the woman facing off with him and clenched his hands to keep them to himself. "If you think I'm going to stand here and listen to a lecture from you..."

"You bet I do! How dare you jeopardize a sick man's health that way," she declared, pointing back toward the Silver Edge. "I don't care what your personal differences are—even you can see he's not well. Yet you lashed out at him with a ruthlessness that was uncalled-for. You can't possibly hold him responsible for the behavior of those men."

"That's what you think. Marsh Keegan may be physically less than what he used to be, but his mind is as shrewd as ever, and that mind is geared for one thing. Power. You can bet either of your licenses he's *always* in control of his men's behavior, Doctor. There isn't a man on the Silver Edge—including that snake Caulfield, or even your boyfriend—who doesn't jump to attention the moment Keegan snaps his fingers."

"Griff is not my boyfriend."

The force of her reply should have placated him some-what, but Navarrone was too furious to notice. "Couldn't tell that from the cozy way you two were standing there."

"This is ridiculous." She tossed her head, whipping her braid back over her shoulder. The movement reminded him of a spirited lioness flicking her tail. "I'm not going to ar-gue with you. I'm only going to reiterate that you should use more discretion in the way you deal with Mr. Keegan—un-less you don't care about being held responsible for the re-sults."

"Is he your patient now?"

"No. As a matter of fact, he politely but firmly threw me out. However, that doesn't change anything. The point is that the man's ill and he doesn't need this kind of excessive harassment."

Navarrone had heard enough. He reached out and, grip-ping her by her upper arms, jerked her so close they were almost nose to nose. "Damn it, are you deaf as well as blind? That man thrives on conflict. He's..."

Whatever else he'd been planning to say vanished from his mind like a teardrop falling on a bed of glowing coals. In its place came awareness, sudden and keen awareness of the woman who was so near his senses were seduced by the bath soap she'd used for her morning shower. That enticingly clean smell, along with seeing the awakening of her own sexuality in her sable-fringed eyes, made short work of the last threads of his self-control.

Dropping his gaze to her parted lips, he knew with a cer-tainty he didn't dare analyze that this woman would be his. He didn't know when; he didn't even know from what side of his genes the ability to foretell that came from or from what ancient culture, only that it was older than any sci-ence or philosophy known to man. And it was real. As the knowledge swept through him, he stiffened against the power of it, trying to keep himself in control. But it was too much. Too soon and too damned much.

Belatedly he realized she was fighting it, as well. Fighting him. All the color was draining from her face. In the end her only defense was to close her eyes.

"Look at me," he demanded thickly. "Don't turn coward now. You feel it as much as I do."

"Let me go," she whispered, still refusing to meet his gaze.

"I don't think so. I think now's as good a time as any to find out exactly what's going on between us and just how deep it's running. Don't tell me you haven't been curious. God, I spent half the night thinking about how you taste."

"I slept like a baby," she tossed back.

He laughed softly and refocused on her mouth. He'd thought it too wide? He'd been wrong. "Liar. You're as tempted as I am to discover what this is all about."

"I already know. You're a bully and I'm—"

"Maddening. At least, you're driving me nuts, and I've known you barely more than twenty-four hours."

"If it's an apology you're after, you have it. Now let go."

She tried to twist free, but that made him determined to draw her all the closer, until his body awoke to the reality of what it was like to have hers completely, stunningly aligned with his.

He drew a long, tension-filled breath. "Slim," he said, "if you do much more of that, we may end up getting arrested ourselves."

Unable to resist, deciding he'd waited long enough, he bent his head, intent on easing at least the sharpest edge of the desire clawing at him. But just as he lowered his lips to hers, she moaned and wrenched away.

"No. Navarrone, don't . . . *please.*

This wasn't the way it was supposed to be. Something was very wrong. Yes, she was trembling, but not from passion. With dawning realization, Navarrone slowly eased his hold—but not completely.

"What is it?" he demanded.

"I—I think I'm going to be sick."

The words were barely audible, but if he had any doubts about what she'd said, they were quickly rejected as she freed herself from his hold—about as subtly as a river bass squirming out of a mountain lion's grasp. She then stumbled away, headed in no particular direction, only needing escape.

Navarrone followed, not because of ego, though it stung bitterly to think that he could have been so wrong, that she could be so repulsed by his touch. Unless she'd been like some of the women he'd encountered in the service—the ones who had charged for their compliments. At least they were honest. There had been women before who wouldn't go out with him because of his ethnic background—or rather, their parents had disapproved—but he'd never made anyone physically ill. No, he told himself as he watched her wrap her arms around her waist. There was something far more troubling going on here.

This was the second time he'd seen her lose it when a man got too close too fast. Considering they'd only met yesterday, that was one time too many to file away as merely coincidence.

"What's wrong with you?" he demanded gruffly, puzzled by her behavior. Did something happen to her down in Central America to make her like this?

"Damn you. Will you leave me *alone?*" she all but screamed back.

He stiffened as though she'd slapped him. All he'd tried to do was help, make up for upsetting her. But maybe he'd read things all wrong.

"Fine," he said, tugging his hat lower on his forehead. He started back toward his truck, intent on giving her what she wanted. Yet his frustration wouldn't let him go. After only a few steps, he wheeled around to face her. "Maybe you are nothing more than a tease. But if so, here's a piece of advice, lady. That game isn't going to play well on Griffin Keegan. His old man won't tolerate a frigid daughter-in-law. He wants grandchildren for the Silver Edge. And soon."

Four

Though he soon regretted his harsh words, Navarrone willed himself to stay away from Erin for the next several days. He needed space, the chance to think rationally, and it was clear the only way he had any success doing that was when she wasn't anywhere within seeing, scenting or touching distance.

Again and again he tried to acknowledge that he would be better off heeding his previous advice to himself. Attraction or no attraction, it was obvious they stood far apart on some important issues. As much as he enjoyed debate and challenge in politics and business, he'd always yearned for a private life patterned after his parents' quietly harmonious partnership. But by the way he and Erin kept striking sparks off each other, it would appear any relationship with her would make harmony a rhetorical question at best. He didn't need that kind of ongoing conflict; he had enough problems as it was.

But space wasn't an easy thing to achieve in a town the size of Azul. No matter how hard they tried to avoid it—and it was soon apparent Erin was holding her own in that department—their paths kept crossing. If he went to Carmelita's, she was there with Wil. When he was checking things out at the post office, she was picking up a package or mailing off a letter.

At first she would ignore him and he her. After a few days, however, he found himself growing hungry for eye contact with her and began to say hello, just to startle her into glancing his way. That soon taught him something new: glances weren't enough.

When a Silver Edge truck began showing up at the Hayes's almost daily, Navarrone reminded himself it wouldn't be there if it wasn't what she wanted. Even so, he kept finding himself checking whenever he drove by the house. And every time he saw the gray pickup, he grew more disturbed. He told himself it was simple concern; after all, there was always a chance that she really didn't know the full story about the Keegans. Wil may not have wanted to come between her friendship with Griff. But he had only to think of Griff's hands on Erin to know full well that what he was experiencing had more to do with red-blooded, wholly masculine jealousy than anything else.

Yet somehow one week managed to pass and then another. News that the clinic was now open for regular hours spread. Area newspapers took notice. On Wednesday of the third week Navarrone unfolded the latest edition of the county paper and noticed a story about Erin on the front page. As he read, it became fairly clear that the reporter had wanted to do a profile on her, but Erin had done her best to focus on the purpose of the clinic and how it would help the residents of Azul and the surrounding area. Yet as he read on, his attention was caught by a brief paragraph mentioning her time in the Peace Corps: "Dr. Hayes served four years in Uruguay and Honduras, where her fiancé, Dr. Paul Forester, was tragically killed during a guerilla raid. Despite the magnitude of her personal loss, Dr. Hayes insisted on completing her tour."

Navarrone shifted his gaze to the photo they'd included of Erin, standing with her grandfather in one of the clinic's examining rooms. Even though the black-and-white photo was gritty, he could see she hadn't been comfortable with all the attention. He, on the other hand, was overwhelmed with new questions.

She'd been engaged. He sat back in his chair and looked out his office window, staring unseeingly at the stooped couple clinging to each other for balance as they shuffled into the Azul State Bank building. He knew it was foolish to be blown away by this latest revelation. Common sense told him it would have been stranger to learn she hadn't had someone in her life. Still, the ramifications multiplied like wakes from a pebble thrown into a pool. She'd loved— deeply enough to make a commitment. She'd also lost that love through violence.

The rippling effect of that disclosure continued. There was more to her story than what she'd told the reporter. Navarrone reread the interview and was convinced of it. In his mind, he began replaying her reaction to him the day he'd tried to kiss her, and he reviewed his recollections of the way she responded when people, men, got too close. An unpleasant feeling began to churn in his stomach. No, he couldn't blame her for not wanting to talk to that reporter, but she would talk to him. He needed to find out the rest of her story, for reasons she couldn't begin to understand. For reasons even he couldn't admit to himself.

He pushed himself to his feet and jerked open his office door. The main room of the police station was relatively quiet, with only Lou Dutton acting as both dispatcher and desk sergeant.

"I'm going out," Navarrone told him, slapping on his hat.

"Pretty late for breakfast," Lou noted, though he didn't look up from the newspaper crossword puzzle he was working on.

"I've already had breakfast."

The hefty policeman glanced up, pushing his glasses back up his short, shiny nose. "You'll be out in your truck then?"

"Maybe."

"Now, Chief, you know if I don't know where you're gonna be, I won't know how to find you if there's an emergency."

Navarrone pulled open the front door and glanced back at him. "Calm down, Lou. This is Azul, not L.A. Besides, if there's trouble, I have a feeling I'll be in the middle of it."

He was parking in the clinic's nearly empty parking lot before he allowed himself to admit he was taking a considerable liberty by coming over here. After all, Erin didn't owe him anything. She would probably see this as just another bad move on his part. But as he stepped up to the front door, he told himself the risk had to be taken.

The freshly painted sign outside the door indicated that the clinic was open, but when he entered the waiting room, he found it vacant except for Teresa Aguilar. Her appearance was one of the many positive things Erin's presence had inspired during the past few weeks. The young widow looked a far cry from the frumpy person she'd allowed herself to become. Today she was wearing a trim, powder blue uniform that flattered her dark complexion. She'd also had her hair cut to chin length, and the style complimented her new professional image. As she glanced up from the typewriter, where she was filling out a medical form, her sloe eyes went wide with surprise.

"Chief Santee—good morning. What... Er, if you've come to see the doctor, she isn't in right now. She's on an emergency call."

He'd noticed the car wasn't outside, but he'd assumed it was Wil who was gone. Now what? he asked himself, not at all used to this feeling of incapacitating indecisiveness.

Before he could thank Teresa and leave, Wil came hurrying from the back of the clinic. He looked hopeful, Navarrone noted wryly.

"I'm here, Teresa. What have we got? Oh. It's you." The twinkle of excitement in Wil's eyes went out like two candle flames doused by a blast from a fire-engine hose. "You don't look like you've been shot or knifed."

"No." He felt the oddest urge to apologize.

Wil shrugged. "I should have known it would be like this when the call came that Sue Sampson was going into early labor. 'Now,' I told myself after Erin left, 'now I'm finally going to get a chance to do some work for a change, without her watching over me like a mother hen.' So what happens? I haven't had a patient all morning."

"That's not true, Dr. Hayes," Teresa scolded gently. "Mr. Jimenez required emergency treatment."

"Pulling a few cactus needles out of Reuben's dimpled backside wasn't what I had in mind. Besides, if he hadn't been drunk, Olivia would have done it for him."

"If he hadn't been drunk, Olivia wouldn't have hit him with her broom and he wouldn't have fallen into her cactus garden," Teresa corrected, barely able to keep a straight face.

"Mmm." Wil ducked his head for a moment. When he looked up at Navarrone again, the twinkle was back in his eyes. "Well, what can we do for you?"

"I . . ." What? What could he say that wouldn't embarrass all three of them? "I can come back some other time."

Wil nodded thoughtfully before doing an about-face and starting back down the hall. "Come with me," he called over his shoulder.

Navarrone hesitated until he saw where the old man was heading—toward the living quarters. Because he thought it might be less embarrassing to leave from the kitchen door, he nodded to Teresa and followed.

"Wait in there," Wil directed, indicating the living room. He went off into the kitchen.

After a brief hesitation, Navarrone removed his hat and did as he'd been told. He'd never been in this part of the house before; the few times he'd visited here, he and Wil had opted to sit at the kitchen table. Wil's reason for altering their routine, however, became clearer when Navarrone noticed the photo of Erin across the room.

He went over to it and picked it up, aware of the quickening of his pulse. She'd been no more than eighteen when it had been taken, and he guessed it was her high school graduation picture. He ran his thumb over the pale skin exposed by her off-the-shoulder gown.

There were several other photos of her around the room: Erin between rounds as an intern, looking exhausted but happy; Erin waving in front of a small plane surrounded by dozens of bronze-skinned laughing children; Erin in a quiet moment sitting beneath the shade of a great tree, a photo undoubtedly taken by someone who'd understood and loved her. Navarrone felt his chest tighten with emotions he decided to analyze later when he was alone.

"You saw the paper."

Navarrone carefully set the picture down. He should have trusted Wil to know exactly what was going on. "I saw the

paper," he murmured, turning to find the physician holding two cans of cola.

"I figured no sense to tempt you if you're on duty."

"Thanks." When he took a can, Wil gestured for him to
have a seat.

"And?" the doctor prompted, easing into his recliner.

Navarrone chose instead to lean against the fireplace
mantel. Another photo of Erin was there. His favorite, he
decided, knowing it would be true no matter how many he
saw of her thereafter. She was lying in a hammock, curled
around the child she was reading to. Both woman and girl
shared the same contented expression, and both looked
ready to drift off to sleep. "And I had no idea of her recent
loss," he said quietly, his gaze on the tender scene. "I've
been hard on her, Wil. I wouldn't have been had I known
her circumstances."

"Why? Didn't she deserve it?"

Navarrone frowned, having expected anything but that
reaction. "I don't follow you."

"If you were hard on her, you obviously had a reason,
right?"

"She's too sympathetic to the Keegans," Navarrone admitted. "Worse, she thinks I'm being unfair to them."

"Are you?" When Navarrone stiffened, Wil made a dis-
missive gesture. "Don't get all bent out of shape. I'm just
trying to get a few things straight. I don't know half of what
you think I do. Rumors. Hearsay. You're a closed book, my
boy, and I've never been one to pry where I wasn't invited.
The only folks left alive who really know your life story are
you and Marsh Keegan."

"But you have your suspicions."

"No. I have my curiosity. However, you should know that
curiosity doesn't have to be satisfied in order for you to talk

about my granddaughter. I didn't bring you back here to barter."

Navarrone exhaled, not realizing until this moment he'd been expecting just that. Still, he felt he owed the old man something for his forthrightness. "Wil, if I told you I don't know the ultimate answer to my own riddle, would you believe me?"

After studying him for a long moment, Wil replied, "Yes. Only I'm not sure that's going to be healthy for my granddaughter. She needs a strong man in her life, a whole man. Not someone who's haunted by a bunch of old ghosts and a taste for vengeance."

He was right, but Navarrone hadn't come here to discuss himself. "I just need to know why she's afraid, Wil."

"Afraid?"

"Of men. Of me." When he noted Wil's unsurprised but mournful reaction, it only depressed him more, because he'd been hoping his instincts were all wrong. "What happened down there? It was there, wasn't it? Did it have anything to do with the guy she was going to marry?"

"Paul. His name was Dr. Paul Forester, and it wasn't him directly. He loved her very much."

"And Erin?"

"She was genuinely fond of him. In her letters she sounded content. Maybe not as deeply in love as I'd always hoped she would be, but they got along extremely well. She once wrote that she thought they would have a compatible marriage."

"Sounds like she had marriage confused with a corporate merger."

"You'd understand her logic if you'd seen the examples she'd had while growing up. Her parents are no shining representation of connubial bliss, and Maury and I . . . Her grandmother was gone before Erin had a chance to see how good it can be between a man and a woman."

Navarrone saw the loneliness in the old man's gaze and felt a pang of commiseration. He'd seen the same look before—in his mother's eyes after his father died. "What happened?" he asked gruffly.

"As the paper said, Erin and Paul were in a mestizo village near the Nicaraguan border when they were attacked by a group of ragtag guerrillas looking for weapons, supplies, whatever. As you've probably read before, those dense mountain forests can be a difficult environment even without political strife. Paul made the mistake of trying to stop them from taking the medicine and food he and Erin had brought for the villagers. They shot him."

As Navarrone stared down into the opening of his soda can, he could almost see the horrific scene. "I was afraid it was something like that."

"It was worse."

"That's enough."

Navarrone knew he was as startled by Erin's appearance in the doorway as Wil was, but her focus was on her grandfather, giving him time to collect himself. He watched the two eye each other and knew that no matter how angry she might be with him, it was nothing compared to her anger at Wil. He fully sympathized with the old man.

"It's my fault, Erin," Navarrone tried to explain. "I pushed."

"Kindly allow me to deal with him myself," she replied, not taking her eyes off her grandfather.

Wil cleared his throat. "How's Mrs. Sampson?"

"It was a false alarm. Would you mind leaving us? Chief Santee and I have something to discuss." She spoke so politely, Wil's ears turned red. "You and I will talk later."

Wil glanced at Navarrone, his expression indicating he wouldn't be looking forward to it. But he rose and left the room without saying another word. When he was gone, Erin turned on Navarrone.

"How dare you!" she seethed, her fingers clenched into fists. "How dare you use him to pry into my personal life!"

"You're right, I should have come directly to you. Actually, I did, only you weren't here and I...I didn't feel I could wait for the answers to my questions."

"Didn't we both make it clear that we have little to say to one another?"

Navarrone's laugh was brief and mirthless. "We tried, but we were both lying. You know it and I know it. Look, Erin—" he took a step toward her "—I came here to mend fences, not hurt you more. Can't you see that?"

"All I can see is that your own inflated ego won't let you accept the fact that someone might not be interested in what you have to offer. I suppose you think if there's something wrong with me, you can let yourself off the hook, is that it? Fine. You want to hear my big dark secret? Listen up."

"Erin, that's not—"

"Everything went completely out of control after Paul was shot," she said, ignoring him. Her voice, huskier than ever, was shaking with pent-up emotion. "The guerrillas began grabbing women and dragging them off to the woods. Two of them got me."

A knifelike spasm went through Navarrone's chest and cut off his breath. "Oh, hell," he rasped.

"Exactly. Pure hell. But I was fortunate. Some men from a neighboring village had heard about us being in the area, and they arrived in time to stop most of it. Once it was safe, I crawled to Paul and tried to do what I could to save him. But he wasn't as lucky as the rest of us. End of story."

Not quite. Somehow she'd found the strength to finish her tour, only to come home and be all but manhandled by him. No wonder she'd almost come out of her skin that day.

And what now? What could he say to her? Could someone whose own life was scarred help another wounded soul? He tried through his job; he tried every day. But that was different. This was more personal. It stunned him to realize how much.

Navarrone set his can on the mantel. His hand was too unsteady to hold it. "Erin..." he began, feeling wholly inadequate.

"Go away," she replied, turning her back to him and wrapping her arms around her waist. "Please. If you have any compassion at all, just get out."

He hesitated, wanting instead to go to her. But she wouldn't welcome his touch, especially not now. And so, because it was what she wanted most, the one thing he could do that would please her, he left.

For days afterward he buried himself in work. He knew that only time could heal this resurgence of Erin's pain. Until then the only useful thing he could do was give her the peace she needed to begin reburying her past. Such a small gesture, and one to which she was no doubt oblivious. It left him feeling very sorry for himself and lonely.

On the third day after he'd heard Erin's story, Navarrone sat in his office snapping the tips off every pencil Lou had sharpened for him. In a fit of disgust, he tossed the latest one across the room. He'd spent the morning reviewing reports and listening to budget complaints from the mayor. Now it was afternoon, and he decided if he didn't get out into the sunlight and clear his head of recycled air soon, he was going to explode.

As he left his office, he heard Hank Baker, another of his officers, grumbling about having to go out in foot patrol. "I'll do it," he said, and walked out before anyone could ask any questions.

It felt good to get outside and let the sun warm his stiff shoulder muscles. Now that it was almost July, the heat chased most residents indoors until the sun was lower on the horizon. But hot and bright had its usefulness.

Up one street and down another he went, pausing to exchange a few words with Ralph Biggs, who'd wandered outside to sweep the sidewalk in front of his market, and Jim Riley, who eyed the area in the hope of finding someone in need of a haircut or shave. Then there was old Mrs. Cantu in widow black, carrying her orange polka-dot umbrella to protect her already-wizened skin from the unforgiving sun.

At the abandoned or unrented stores, he paused to check for forced entry and vandalism. He was coming out of one such entryway when a blur of blond curls in a red playsuit rushed past him and tripped over an uneven slab of cement.

"Whoa, sunshine!" He'd had to move fast, but he caught her before her bare knees hit the ground. "Where's the fire?"

Five-year-old Missy Colton, daughter of the pleasant couple who owned the fabric and sewing-machine store, giggled and gazed up at him from beneath overgrown toffee-colored bangs. "There's no fire, Chief Santee. Momma gave me money for an ice cream and I gotta go get it."

"I've just been by the market myself and I know for a fact that they've got plenty of ice cream, so how about slowing down. You don't want to scrape those pretty knees, do you?"

The child bent from the waist to stare wonderingly down at her limbs. ''Billy says I have chicken legs.''

''What does your brother know? He's only four. Trust me, lovebug, in a few more years, you're going to turn heads all the way up and down this street, okay?''

Enthralled with the idea, the child nodded. '''Bye, Chief.''

'''Bye, kiddo.''

Still hunched down, he watched her sashay the rest of the way to her destination. Women, he thought. If only the one haunting his dreams was so easy to reach.

''You're very good with children. Why does that surprise me?''

At the sound of her voice, Navarrone had the strangest feeling the ground shifted under his feet, but it didn't keep him from pivoting to face her. She stood only a few feet away. Glancing up the length of her yellow slacks and white-and-yellow tank top, he thought she looked as cool and fresh as lemon sherbert, despite that fatigue shadowing her eyes.

''I'll bite. Why does that surprise you?'' he murmured, finally rising. God, she was lovely, he thought. This was the first time he'd seen her with her hair loose, and all he could think of was how much he wanted to touch it, touch her.

''You don't seem the type,'' she said with a shrug.

''Just because I don't have any kids doesn't mean I wouldn't like some.''

''What's stopping you?''

''An agreeable woman.''

Erin lifted an eyebrow and he could see she was fighting her amusement. ''Don't try to tell me you haven't been able to find one of those, even in a small town like this.''

''I'm flattered you still think it should be easy for me,'' he replied, resting a shoulder against the plate-glass window of the store he'd just checked. He hoped it made him appear less tense than he actually felt. "Unfortunately—or maybe fortunately—that's not the case. At any rate, I'm a firm believer in fate. If you were meant to fall in love, then you're going to meet that person whether you're in a city with a million other people or a town with a few dozen. I'm patient," he added with a coaxing smile.

She didn't return the smile, and silence descended between them. "I'd better be going," Erin finally murmured, fiddling with the pharmacy bag in her hands. "Amelia Crow is waiting for me. She's still not doing well with that broken hip. I thought I'd check on her while I bring her this refill of painkillers."

"Nice lady."

"She is. Very."

"I meant you."

She didn't seem to know how to react to that. Her bewildered expression threatened to make the spontaneous tenderness rising in Navarrone uncontainable. "Cat's got your tongue, Slim."

She shook her head as though denying more than his words. "I really need to be going."

"You're pushing it pretty hard these days."

"My job is to be available when people need me."

No one had been more surprised or impressed than he at how quickly the residents were coming to accept and trust her. "Calm down. I've just been concerned about you. Is that such an unwelcome thought?"

"It depends on what it's ultimately going to cost me."

Navarrone smiled more easily this time and let his gaze wander over her face. When he got to her mouth, hunger made him flex the muscles of his abdomen. "Slim, you're a tough woman to break through to."

"I wish you wouldn't call me that."

"Why not? I've decided it suits you. Want to know when? Weeks ago. The moment I first learned what it feels like to hold your body against mine."

"Is that your idea of humor?" Erin asked stiffly.

"If you weren't so afraid to look lower than my badge right now, you'd see that I'm feeling anything but humorous," he muttered. Damn, he thought a moment later when he saw her expression turn icy. How could he say that when the last thing she wanted to deal with at this point was sex? But how could he make her understand that it was virtually impossible for him to shut off his attraction to her? She might be feeling less than desirable, but he was beginning to realize he'd never met another woman he wanted more. "Erin," he said urgently, "I know what happened has been hard for you to deal with, but there's nothing for you to be ashamed of."

"Ashamed?" she whispered raggedly. "A good man, a *kind* man, died before my eyes, and I didn't do anything to save him because I was terrified, scared to death and wanting to save my own skin."

Navarrone exhaled, understanding the agony of that no-win kind of torment. "There was nothing you could have done. Do you think you would feel better today if those animals had had time to finish the job they'd started on you?"

"You don't know anything about how I feel or would have felt."

As she started around him again, Navarrone grabbed her arm. He knew it was risky. Unpopulated as this block was, they were still on a public street, and she was vulnerable. The timing for this couldn't be worse. But he was beyond caring about timing or unwanted spectators. "I understand more than you might realize," he insisted, fighting to keep his own emotions in check.

"Look." She wrenched herself free. "I'm sorry about your friend getting killed, but—"

"I'm not talking about Fred, I'm talking about my mother," he ground out. "She was raped, Erin."

Five

She shouldn't have run away. In the days following Navarrone's shocking admission, that was the one truth that kept coming back to Erin. She should have stayed, said something, listened. As a doctor and a woman, she better than most should have been sensitive to what such honesty had cost him. But the all-too-human, wounded side of her had been hit with too much. Staying would have been a challenge even for the physician; for the victim, it had been an impossibility.

She should, however, have anticipated that it wouldn't stop her mind from churning out endless questions. Navarrone's mother. The poor woman. How had it happened? When? Who? Her mind grew feverish from the thoughts racing through it—except for one. Why? *Why?* was what a survivor quickly learned to stop asking. If you didn't, it would consume you, drive you over the brink for one simple reason: there was no answer to *why* except *because.*

How many years had he been living with this? Too many. She could sense that much. In fact, many things were becoming increasingly clear. She felt as if he'd given her a piece to a troublesome jigsaw puzzle, and as often happens with such things, the piece had spawned a watershed reaction. Other bits of information were beginning to make sense, patterns were slipping into place. It was suddenly reasonable why he'd reacted with such violence the morning in the café when Griff startled her; she now understood the sadness she often saw shadowing his dark eyes; she had a new level of appreciation for the way he'd tried to harness his physical attraction toward her. There were so many times when she should have been more understanding, when she should have shown more compassion. But what had she done? She'd accused him of being insensitive, and in the one moment he'd shared the darkest corner of his soul with her, she'd beat a fast retreat.

How she must have hurt him. How they had hurt each other. Where did they go from here? He hadn't been wrong, she was unbelievably drawn to him. She was even beginning to realize that in Navarrone Santee she'd found the one man who could take her beyond her old doubts, fears and humiliation. At least, her body insisted it was so. Her mind, however, refused to let her forget that in practically every other area—beginning with her friendship with Griff Keegan—they faced some overwhelming conflicts.

"Doctor? Erin?"

Erin blinked and realized Teresa was before her in the clinic's hallway, a frown of concern puckering her wide forehead. Small wonder, she thought, glancing down to see the memo pad the young woman had been trying to hand her. How long had she been standing there in a trance?

"Excuse me." She offered a quick grimace as she accepted the pad and handed over the file on the patient she'd just finished with. "I guess I'm a bit preoccupied."

"For days now. Are you not feeling well?"

"No, of course not. I mean, I'm fine."

"You don't look it. You look troubled, and I don't think you've been sleeping as much as you should, either."

Erin maneuvered so she could put an arm around the shorter woman's shoulders. The past several weeks had given her ample opportunity to get to know Teresa better and to discover what a warm and caring person she was. She'd also learned that Teresa's mothering instincts didn't stop with her children.

"I admit I've had a lot on my mind," she told her, giving her an appreciative hug. "But I duly note that I'm slipping and promise to straighten up, okay?"

"I'll believe it when I see it. It wouldn't hurt you to remember to eat once in a while, too. An extra helping of *huevos* for breakfast and some *frijoles* with dinner will stop Dr. Wil from calling you a sparrow wing."

And Navarrone from calling her "Slim," Erin thought, feeling a strange quickening within her as she was once again reminded of him. Giving herself a mental shake, she recited, "Eggs are loaded with cholesterol, and that's a four-letter word in a doctor's vocabulary. And," she added, with a rueful smile, "after four years in the Corps, I've had enough beans to last me a lifetime. Now, what's this address for?"

"It was a small practice east of Lemitar, belonging to a Dr. Simpson. He's retiring, and he said he'd read about you in the paper and thinks you could use a good deal of his equipment."

"Oh, Teresa, you know our financial situation. We're in no condition to buy anything yet, except for the basic—"

"Not buy," Teresa corrected. "He wants to *give* you these things."

They'd wandered back into the office she shared with her grandfather. He was there, sitting behind the desk muttering to himself as he peered down at the folder before them. "Teresa, I don't know what this says."

"You must. You wrote it."

"Five years ago! Even an elephant wouldn't be able to remember that far back."

"Even an elephant would have better penmanship than yours."

He sat back in his chair and glared at her. "I liked you better when you were my cleaning lady, and I *don't* like doing this. This isn't work. Updating files—punishment's what it is." He focused on Erin. "I'm a doctor, confound it. I may be getting old, but I'm not senile!"

Erin sat down on the edge of the desk and rubbed her forehead. His continuing insistence on taking on more of a work load was becoming an increasingly sensitive matter between them. She thought he would enjoy his semiretirement, knowing she was there to bear the brunt of responsibility for the practice, and she wanted to provide this for him, because she loved him and was grateful for all the years he'd helped her. But apparently he wasn't interested in relaxing completely.

"Could we table the dissension for now, Gramps? Tell me about this Dr. Simpson. Do you know him?"

"Of course I know him. The old coot's five years older'n me and looks twice that. Now if you want to hear about someone who's going senile . . ."

"What I want to know is, do you think his offer is legitimate?"

"No doubt. It sounds crazy enough. Of course, the only way you're going to find out is to drive up there and talk to him."

Erin glanced down at the pad. "He wants me to come out today, but that's impossible. I have appointments."

"I can take care of those." When Erin opened her mouth to protest, he raised his hand. "I'm putting my foot down on this. You've coddled me and babied me and done everything but put me in a nursing home, Erin. It's got to stop. I may not be spry enough to race Teresa here up and down the hallway, but hell's fire, I can still take an accurate blood-pressure reading and a few other things. It's not as though I'm going to forget almost forty years of medicine in a few hours."

Erin bit her lip. Had she been that bad? She'd never meant for him to feel he wasn't trusted—or needed. Heaven knew, she was beginning to see she would soon require some help, and who better than the man who knew how she operated and vice versa? Besides, if Dr. Simpson's offer was half as good as it sounded, she couldn't afford *not* to go see him.

"All right," she said slowly. "If that's how you feel, we'll try it. This afternoon's caseload is yours—under one condition."

"What's that?"

"Teresa takes all the notes. Gramps, she's right. Your handwriting really is atrocious."

"Mind if I sit down, or were you about to leave?"

Navarrone looked up from the salt- and pepper shakers he'd been fiddling with to find Sheriff Kyle Langtry standing beside his booth. With a cursory tilt of his head, he invited the middle-aged man to take the seat across from him.

"Rough day?" the bespectacled, burnished-haired officer asked.

Rough week, Navarrone amended silently, and he didn't see things improving, since there hadn't been any sign that Erin was ready or willing to talk to him. He was beginning to think it was time to face reality: the lady didn't want anything to do with him.

"I've seen better," he replied as the man hung his hat on the booth's post and sat down. "You look like you've skirted a few mine fields yourself. What's wrong? Did your wife kick you out of the wrong side of bed this morning?"

"I wish she had. At least there would be making up to look forward to. No, I'm here to pass on some bad news."

Navarrone silently prepared himself for the worst. Lately, all he seemed to be hearing was bad news. Lou bashed in the passenger door of his patrol car; some kids almost burned down cranky Mrs. Hillary's Lady's Emporium while indulging in an anticipatory July Fourth fireworks display; and the mayor wanted to cut his department's budget in order to have the funds to build a "Welcome to Azul" monument near the interstate. Then, of course, there was Erin.

Out of the corner of his eye, he spotted Carmelita signaling him. "Carmelita wants to know if you want to order," he said to Kyle.

"Can't." Kyle turned around and gave her a combination wave and shake of his head. "I still have a few stops to make before I can call it a day," he said, once again facing Navarrone.

"Sounds like trouble, all right. Well, let's have it."

The other man took another moment to glance around the room before bowing his head over his loosely linked hands. "A couple more horses have been found."

Whatever appetite Navarrone had vanished with his friend's reluctant statement. Anger took its place, causing his whole body to tense until he thought his spine might snap. He slumped back in his seat. "Where?"

"Nowhere near Keegan land, so at least you can relax about that."

"Where?"

"Twenty miles northwest. A group of tourists, amateur treasure hunters, found the carcasses—or what was left of them. It'd been several days," Kyle said, his voice apologetic when Navarrone was unable to repress a grimace. "I left a couple men to continue scoping the area. I'm hoping they'll find some casings to go with the ones we recovered from the other sights."

"They will," Navarrone replied, staring through the man across from him as though he weren't there. "The guy who's doing this wants them to know he used a .340 Weatherby Magnum and that it'll be untraceable. I think it gives him a kick."

"Right now I'd settle for knowing what would make a person use a bullet with such damage potential like that. Those things would take down a buffalo on amphetamines."

"Or a horse you wanted to be sure stayed down on the first hit."

"That's sick." Kyle shifted, rested his elbows on the table and pressed his clasped hands to his compressed lips. "You're still sticking with the theory that Marsh Keegan's behind this, aren't you?"

"Oh, he's behind it all right. If he wasn't confined to that wheelchair, he'd be out there pulling the trigger himself."

"You're making a dangerous accusation, my friend."

"You've said that before, but who else around here can afford a rifle that costs over thirteen hundred dollars? I'll tell you—a person who doesn't care that he can't risk displaying it in his gun cabinet. A person who doesn't mind driving to a big city for ammunition because a local can't afford to stock that caliber for one customer. A man who's calculated this with the cool head of a strategist."

The sheriff dragged off his glasses and rubbed at his face. "It still doesn't make sense, damn it! He'd be gambling everything he's built."

"And don't think for a moment he's not getting great satisfaction in taking that gamble. What's more, he's going to continue killing, because most people share your skepticism. Do you know what riles me the most?" Navarrone asked, looking Kyle straight in the eye. "No one really cares. Until Fred was killed, the media was all but apathetic about the situation, and things haven't changed much, have they? Who's going to miss a vagrant Indian or a few horses that don't belong to anyone? They only care when something affects their wallets, like this year's rainfall being even lower than normal, grazing land suffering as a result or feed prices going up."

"I guess I just haven't wanted to see that," Kyle confessed, though he looked anything but happy about having to do so now.

"Finally, don't forget," Navarrone concluded, leaning closer to keep his voice low, "Keegan yelled louder than anyone when the BLM guys said there wasn't sufficient funds budgeted to deal long term with the growing herds. Didn't he say right into a reporter's mike that he thought the big showy roundup the government held was purely a con job for the news media? That it was time the taxpayers took matters into their own hands?"

The sheriff touched the badge on his chest before running his hand down to his stomach. "I'm getting too old for this job," he muttered.

Though Navarrone commiserated with him, he remained firm in his convictions. "If you'd get past the notion that a man who's dined with the governor could be behind something this dirty, you'd agree that I'm making sense, Kyle.''

"I *am*. At least, I'm beginning to. That's what's scaring me.'' Moving with more weariness than when he sat down, Kyle Langtry pushed himself to his feet. "I've gotta go, but I'll keep you informed.''

"I appreciate that.''

The older man squeezed Navarrone's shoulder before retrieving his hat and then, sighing, he left.

Once again alone, Navarrone sat thinking that now he knew what a gutted deer felt like. Drained of everything except frustration and bitterness, the walls of the café seemed to close in on him. He had to move. He had to get out into the fresh air and away from the chatter of the early evening crowd.

Only when he came up to the counter did he consider how Carmelita would take his premature departure. One glance and she placed her hands on her voluptuous hips. "I'm gonna guess. You're canceling your order? This is the second time in a month that you've done this to me.''

"I'm aware of that,'' he replied, reaching into his back pocket. "That's why I intend to pay you this time.''

"Pay—bah! You think it's the money? It's my reputation! What are people supposed to think when it gets around town that the chief of police loses his appetite whenever he comes to Carmelita's, eh?''

Navarrone opened his mouth to offer another apology. That was when he spotted the glimmer in her eye. It struck him that she could tell he was upset and was trying to tease him into smiling. Grateful, but still only able to manage something closer to a grimace, he replied, "I promise I'll do better next time.''

"Sure, sure. Put that away.'' She flicked her dish towel at his billfold. "What are you doing? Insulting me again?''

"You're a good lady, Carmelita."

"And you're a pain in the part of me a lady doesn't mention in mixed company."

The sun was sinking fast when Erin turned off the interstate at the exit just before Azul. There was an alternate route she wanted to take that would allow her to enjoy a more scenic drive. It was a few miles farther from home, but that was fine. And once she got to the house, she was going to cook herself and Gramps a special dinner, a celebratory dinner. She'd even stopped in Socorro to pick up a few things, including a bottle of chardonnay.

She'd been smiling to herself ever since she'd left Dr. Claude Simpson's clinic. For once she hadn't had to negotiate, wheedle or beg for her patients. The man's offer had been a dream; he'd truly wanted his equipment and treatment aids passed on to a place they were needed. Arrangements had been made. Everything would be freighted over within the next two weeks. Dr. Simpson was even picking up the shipping charges.

Yes, it had been a trip worth making, she thought, turning off the air-conditioning and rolling down the window. She drew a deep breath, filling her lungs with the hot arid air, and tilted her head toward the window to let the wind tug playfully at her hair. She'd released it from its barrette when she'd changed into the simple floral-print sundress for the drive. For the first time in months, she wasn't consumed by guilt for being alive or for feeling happy. For the first time in months, it felt good to be young and attractive.

She was humming one of Teresa's favorite songs when she made the final turn toward Azul. As she topped a small hill, she could see the white picket fence of the town cemetery on the next rise. The neat structure and U-shaped line of pition that provided the only protection against the elements for the headstones looked out of place, yet serene amid their more barren surroundings. When she was parallel to it, she glanced at the marble statue of the angel that had kept watch over the area since Azul was first settled. But her view was blocked by a white Ramcharger—a truck identifiable by its overhead lights and siren.

Erin hit the brakes before she realized she'd made a conscious decision to do so. The screech of the old station wagon's tires sliding on pavement made the man sitting on the grass glance over his shoulder. Had he been in a different vehicle, Erin would still have been able to tell by his silhouette, by the way his cowboy hat was tilted low over his forehead, that he was Navarrone.

Her heart began to pound as though she'd been sprinting. Her hands gripped the steering wheel in a strangling clench. She was too far away to actually read his expression, but she felt the power of his gaze as intensely as if they'd been standing toe-to-toe. *Lonely* was the word that came to mind. He looked like the loneliest man on earth sitting there between those two graves.

For an instant she resented that, resented him. She wanted to recapture her happy mood, the aura of contentment she'd been basking in. She didn't want to deal with all the tumultuous emotions he kept igniting in her. Couldn't she have at least a few hours of peace?

Then he turned away.

It stung.

Damn him, Erin thought, swallowing to ease the lump that ached in her throat. Why should she be overwhelmed with guilt?

Shame followed on the heels of that. It chilled her skin, and even as she shivered, she shifted the station wagon into reverse and backed up several yards. Then she turned into the cemetery's gravel driveway.

By the time she parked behind his truck and shut off the car engine, the combination of nerves and heat had droplets of perspiration trickling down her spine. What did you say to someone you'd been avoiding for days? As she got out and approached him, she wondered and worried. It didn't help that he wasn't making any move to acknowledge her presence. That only made her more nervous—though she felt he had every right to reject her. When he took a deep breath, she watched the material of his blue shirt draw tightly across his broad back. This was not, she reminded herself, the time to dwell on how muscular he was or how it felt to be held by him.

Once at his side, she saw he'd been toying with a blade of grass. He drew it one last time through his fingers before dropping it between his upraised knees. "I come here when I need to think."

His words were directed at her, but he continued to focus on the piñon trees. Erin wet her dry lips. If intimidation had been his intent, he couldn't have begun with a better opening line. "Are you saying you want me to leave?"

"It might be a good idea if you're planning to run away from me again the moment things begin to get complicated."

No, she thought, he wouldn't make it easy for her. But then, the most important, the most worthwhile things never were.

With a new sense of resolve, Erin lowered herself to the sun-warmed carpet of fragrant grass. "When I'm dealing with a problem," she replied, following his gaze to the tree line, "I withdraw from everyone and everything but my work."

Out of the corner of her eye, she spotted a muscle flex along his strong jaw. Silence lingered between them for another moment. Then, just when she was beginning to wonder if she was going to have to apologize outright, he gestured at the two headstones before him. "My parents were both proud, stubborn people, yet they were together for nineteen years. I rarely heard them raise their voices at one another."

Erin considered the simple, rose-marble headstones that bore the names of his parents, James Clay Santee and Anna Estevez Santee. She'd noticed them a few weeks ago when she'd driven Teresa here to bring flowers to her husband's grave, but only now did she realize by the dates carved beneath that Navarrone's mother had died sixteen years ago, three years to the day after his father.

Questions filled Erin's mind, but she knew this wasn't the proper time for them. She was here to help the living, the man beside her and maybe even herself.

She turned to Navarrone. Beneath the shadow of his hat, his bronzed, strong-boned face was drawn. Deep lines cut into the skin around his eyes and mouth like scars. He looked exhausted, emotionally and spiritually drained. But what was most poignant to Erin was seeing his bloodshot eyes. He looked like a man who needed to weep, but could not.

Erin glanced from him to the markers and back again, beginning to comprehend. He'd been born in the shadow of a great love, and no one could replace what he'd lost. What could she possibly do to make the void in his life more bearable?

"If you need to talk," she said, fighting to keep the tremor out of her voice, "I'll listen."

"After the way we parted the other day, I thought you'd never allow yourself to get within a mile of me again."

"It just goes to show you . . . life is full of surprises."

This time he looked, and his gaze drifted over her face, her hair, her dress. "Or else I'm dreaming. I was beginning to believe I'd forgotten how."

As intense as his eyes were, they seemed to be looking from a place far away. Something nagged at Erin. "Navarrone . . . what's happened? Something has, I can feel it."

"Something's always happening. Death. Life. Chaos. But you don't look like you've had a normal day," he added, his expression softening. "You look very pleased with yourself and . . . very lovely."

The words sent a thrill through her body, giving her goose bumps despite her growing concern for him. "I am pleased," she replied, deciding to tell him where she'd just come from and why.

His answering smile seemed to radiate from his soul. "A woman of quiet force," he murmured.

Because she was captivated by the dark fire in his eyes, she wasn't sure she'd heard him correctly. "I don't understand."

"That's what my mother would have called you. She came from a family who had a great respect for individuals of strong principle and direction, particularly when they were women. My mother was a strong woman herself. Strange how it's often the most sensitive, the most fragile looking, who are."

The taut pain in his voice caused a corresponding ache in Erin's chest. Though she still didn't quite dare to touch him while he was in this strange mood, she found herself unable to resist leaning closer. "Please. I know I haven't given you much cause to put your faith in me, but I'm asking for another chance. Tell me what's tormenting you so."

"Kyle Langtry came to see me today."

The sheriff's name almost had her catching her breath in anticipation—why, she wasn't sure. "And?"

"Two more horses have been found."

He was being kind via omission. She could see it by the vein throbbing beside his eye and the tension around his mouth. Because she knew no words of sympathy would mean enough, she gave him the gift of time to control his rage before repeating gently, "And?"

"And as before, there don't seem to be any really useful leads, so it will happen again. Then again. Until someone either more socially prominent than an Indian gets shot or the entire population of wild horses is wiped off the face of the earth."

"Are you upset because of the shootings, or because the sheriff isn't as convinced as you are that it's someone from the Silver Edge who's involved?"

His sharp look tempted her to run back to her car and lock the doors. "Marsh Keegan is involved. Don't ever doubt it, Erin."

"Don't look at me that way. I'm not totally rejecting the idea, really I'm not. But in all honesty..."

"Would you find it easier to believe if I told you that the man you're giving the benefit of the doubt to is the same man who raped my mother?"

Erin stared, for a moment not sure she'd heard him correctly. "Dear God," she finally whispered, exhaling shakily.

"He denied that incident, too," Navarrone continued, years of bitterness beginning to rush to the surface. "She was barely twenty and in love. Things looked good. My father had recently been accepted by the state police. They were getting close to setting a date for their wedding." He turned to the stones, whose chiseled edges sparkled in the waning sunlight. "He'd known Mother wasn't comfortable working at the ranch. Keegan's first wife had died several years before, and it was no secret among the staff that the SOB had cornered her a few times while she'd been away from everyone, vulnerable. But she refused to quit or be intimidated. It had gotten to be a point of principle with her. Besides that, she'd wanted to be a full partner in her marriage, do her share in setting up her new home.''

His harsh, monotone delivery was almost harder to take than rage would have been. Erin wanted to press her hands to her ears, scream, but she forced herself to do neither. How had he discovered all this? she wondered. Who could be so cruel as to tell him such painful details?

As if he could read her mind, he said, "I learned about it when I was in grade school. For the first several years after my parents married, we lived north of here. My father had gotten a transfer. But later, after he was promoted, they had to move back. My father didn't want to take the job at first, but my mother insisted.

"There was a kid in my class who lived on the Silver Edge, and his father remembered my mother. The kid thought it would be fun to repeat what he'd heard at home and dutifully informed me of what I was. Up until then I barely knew what the word 'bastard' meant, let alone bothered with the mathematics regarding my birth. But that day I went home and asked why I was born only seven months after my parents married.''

Erin knew he was trying for a self-deprecating tone, and that made it all the more difficult to listen to him. Besides, Anna's story came too close to her own nightmare. "Are you saying your father is really...?''

"Suddenly his name isn't so easy to say, is it?'' he drawled, though his knuckles were turning white from the way he was clenching his hands. Then the bitter irony vanished and in its place was sheer desolation. "I don't know what he is to me. I asked my mother. Twice. Both times she denied it. But after her death, I found an envelope she'd left for me among her things. It's at home, still unopened. You see, Erin, I'm not sure I want to find out what's inside. If I ever did discover Marsh Keegan's my father...I think I'd have to kill him.''

Six

———

Erin whispered Navarrone's name. Her heart ached for the injustices his mother had suffered, injustices her son still bore for her on his own soul. Here was a man who was living proof that past sins were not subject to any statute of limitations; they honored no time boundaries; their backlash was indiscriminate.

Half expecting to be rebuffed, but knowing she couldn't let it stop her if he tried, she touched his shoulder. He stiffened, and once again she saw the muscles along his powerful, proud jaw work tensely. Yet, to her relief, he didn't push her away. It was enough to give her the courage to lean forward until she was resting her head against his shoulder.

Beneath her cheeks, his chest rose and fell. When she felt his fingers at her hair, his touch was as hesitant as hers had been entreating. "Is this pity?" he asked her, his voice ragged. "I wasn't asking for any."

"No."

He fell silent again and Erin waited. Like a midwinter thaw, the tension slowly eased out of him. His breathing quieted. Her heartbeat calmed to a steady, strong beat. With a sigh that spoke fathoms, he turned to press his face against her hair.

"You smell like spring and dreams," he breathed, stroking his cheek up and down. "God, Erin...I don't know why you're trusting me, giving to me this generously, but don't stop. I'm so empty inside. Don't stop."

"Shh." Shifting, Erin wrapped her arms around him. The embrace had less to do with sexuality—though it was impossible for the man not to affect her on that level—and more to do with compassion. Gently she rocked him, stroked the hair at his nape, his rigid shoulder muscles, his back. Her ministrations weren't unlike those of a mother soothing a child, though destiny had stolen Navarrone's childhood long before he'd been born. She was convinced, though, that beneath his scars a hurt and confused little boy still existed.

She had no idea how long they stayed that way, but ultimately realized his hands had fallen to his sides and were gripping handfuls of grass to keep himself from clutching and...frightening her? Nothing else he could have said or done could have reached under her defenses more poignantly.

"Come home with me, Navarrone," she said softly, easing back to look into his eyes. "You need to get away from here. It's time to be around the living."

"You've done enough."

"No, I haven't. Besides, you need a home-cooked meal...and people to get your mind off all this."

"Slim, I don't think I'd be very good around people right now."

Hearing her nickname once again roll off his tongue buoyed Erin with new conviction. "It's just going to be me and Gramps. You don't have to put on a front for us."

He cocked an eyebrow. "You said home-cooked?"

She let a hint of laughter creep into her voice, every minute growing more and more convinced she wanted to take a risk with this man. "Pretty basic fare, though. Steak, baked potatoes and as close to a Caesar salad as my culinary skills allow. In case it doesn't work out, I also have a respectable chardonnay to appease the palate." When she saw temptation flicker in his eyes, she stood and extended her hands to him, aware that not since Paul had she willingly invited a man's touch who was not related to her. "Come home with me, Navarrone."

It seemed an eternity before he finally closed his fingers around hers. It would have been impossible for her to remain ignorant of the differences between them. His hands were so much larger, so much darker than hers, and his skin was far more callused and rough. But what Erin was most sensitive to was the gentleness he had inside, which was as reassuring as it was surprising.

He rose, graceful despite his fatigue, and gazed down at her. "You're sure?"

If she hadn't been, his wistfulness would have convinced her. Smiling, she led him toward their cars.

There was no doubt her grandfather was surprised to see her walk in with Navarrone in tow, but, Erin noted gratefully, he covered it well. Within minutes of their arrival, the two men were sitting at the dinette table drinking beer—both wasted no time declining her wine—and reaching for the cheese and crackers she set out for them. Erin prepared the rest of their dinner while blissfully enjoying a glass of her chardonnay.

"So what did you think of Simpson?" her grandfather asked her after a few minutes of small talk.

"He seemed a sweet and funny man, but you were right about him. His wife walked me out later and told me he'd been diagnosed with Alzheimer's. They're going to be moving in with her sister, who has a big place in Sante Fe. It has a reliable nursing home within walking distance. Fortunately money isn't going to be a problem for them."

Her grandfather shook his head. "An amazing situation—and all because of one newspaper interview."

"I have a feeling there aren't too many people who remain unmoved by Erin once they've met her," Navarrone countered.

Pleasure was a warm honey running through her veins until Erin felt the heat flooding her cheeks and caught the look of shrewd speculation in her grandfather's eyes. "Gramps deserves a lot of credit in this case. If he hadn't been available to take my patients this afternoon, I couldn't have afforded to take the time off. How did it go?" she asked him.

"Fine. Great. I can take over most of the follow-ups like you had today. That would give you more time to deal with emergencies and things."

Erin hid her smile by bending to turn the steaks in the broiler. "We'll see."

That earned her a snort of frustration. "There's a tidy rejection if I ever heard one." He leaned toward Navarrone. "She's been perfecting that tone since she was no taller than this table. Biggest mistake I ever made was admitting it was cute. But how was I to know she'd grow up to have the strategy techniques of a military field marshal?"

Unperturbed, Erin checked on the potatoes in the microwave. She knew he was only teasing. For the most part, she amended, with an inward chuckle. At any rate, his dry wit was exactly what Navarrone needed to get his mind off himself and his troubles.

As she washed the vegetables she'd purchased for the salad, her grandfather continued talking, and she occasionally added a comment or observation to keep him from indulging in too much creative license. But otherwise she remained silent, which allowed her more opportunity to covertly study Navarrone and think about the latest revelations he'd shared with her.

On one level her mind was still reeling from shock. Marsh Keegan, a rapist. Though she'd never been able to feel the fondness for him that she did for Griff, the sheer magnitude of his offense was difficult to come to terms with. How could he have forced himself on someone who not only was an employee in his home and had relied on and trusted his decency, but who'd been in love with another person? It showed such a lack of compassion, such violence.

Then she tried to deal with the reality that Navarrone could be Marsh Keegan's son. She now understood why Navarrone's dramatic face often possessed an expression of barely leashed rage. If she'd been the one carrying this knowledge all these years, could she have borne it without somehow erupting? Could she have been able to return to Azul, or—filled with loathing at the mere thought of having to look at the instigator of her despair—would she have been compelled to stay away?

Erin's heart ached for all the Santees. No wonder Navarrone wanted Marsh Keegan indicted for the shootings. It couldn't change the past or redeem it, but it would be a salve on old wounds. Conversely, as guilty as Marsh might be for one crime, was it just to punish him for another without indisputable proof?

"If you stir that much harder, you're going to carve a hole in the bottom of the bowl," Navarrone whispered in her ear, as he reached around her to swipe a sliver of Parmesan cheese.

His unexpected nearness gave Erin a jolt, but she saw he was right; she was stirring the ingredients for the salad dressing with almost comical ruthlessness. A glance to see the intense attention her grandfather was giving the task of setting the table told her that he, too, had noticed.

She cleared her throat. "Thanks for the warning. I'd hate to ruin a matching set."

"My pleasure. Anything else I can do? Considering the way my stomach is beginning to growl, I think taste testing is definitely up my alley."

Unable to resist, Erin offered him one of the as-yet-unchopped anchovies. "Here."

With a playful scowl, he captured her wrist and directed her to drop the fish. Then he navigated that same finger to the bowl, where he dipped it into the mixture of lemon juice, olive oil, garlic and pepper, and lifted it to his mouth. "Mmm. Tangy yet sweet."

"Sweet?" She knew her mimicry sounded inane, but her brain had shifted into neutral and her heart was thrumming from the warm, wet stroking of his tongue. "It can't be. There's no, uh, sugar in this recipe."

"Well, unless you're planning to feed us by hand, maybe there should be."

Before she could think of an appropriate comeback, he left her to rejoin her grandfather.

"I'm as full as a tick," Wil said for the second time since rising from the dinner table.

They'd adjourned to the living room where the mood had gone from comfortably chatty to comfortably lethargic, while they lingered over second cups of coffee and snifters of the special cognac Wil kept for occasions.

Erin eyed her grandfather rocking in his recliner beside her. "You can stop hinting," she told him drolly. "I wasn't going to ask you to help me with the dishes."

"I'll help," Navarrone said, swirling his cognac. From his spot on the couch, he still looked tired, but the lines of strain were easing, particularly around his mouth.

"Of course you won't," Erin replied, sensitive to her inclination to stare at him entirely too much.

Her grandfather glanced up from the pipe he'd been filling. "If you ask me, a man's got the right to feel he's done his part, if he's so inclined."

"No one's asking you," she replied sweetly.

"Impudence." Stabbing the stem of his pipe into his mouth, he rose and stretched. After shooting their guest a wink he didn't try to hide from Erin, he announced, "When she gets this way, it's my cue to run for cover. Self-preservation, my boy. The true secret to longevity."

"Gramps, it's barely after nine," Erin pointed out, her impulse battling with her anxieties. On the one hand she would like a chance to be alone with Navarrone; on the other, she was concerned he could see through her grandfather's machinations and be embarrassed.

"Good. That means I'll get to have my smoke and read a chapter or two before I shut off my light. Night, children."

Mortified, Erin stared into her own snifter and listened to every one of his footsteps as he climbed the stairs. She compared them to a drumroll at an execution. Only when she heard his bedroom door click shut could she bring herself to lift her gaze—and found herself meeting Navarrone's equally somber scrutiny.

"Now you know why he chose medicine over a stage career," she said.

He remained silent.

Lovely. You bring the man home and haven't a clue as to what to do with him.

After a few seconds—just long enough for Erin's nerves to fray to tethered wisps—he stood and, collecting Wil's glassware and china, beckoned her with a tilt of his head. So much for that, Erin thought, retrieving the coffee tray bearing the rest of their things. With a sigh, she followed him dutifully to the kitchen.

There she found him already filling the dishpan with hot water. "Oh, no," she said, setting the tray on the kitchen table. "I was serious. You're not going to do that."

"You can dry, since I don't know where anything goes."

"There's not that much to clean up. I can do this later. It won't take me more than fifteen minutes or so."

He shut off the water with such force that the pipes shuddered in protest. Paying them little heed, he grasped her by her upper arms. "Do you want me to leave?"

"No."

"Honestly?"

"*No.*"

"I'm trying to make you relax around me."

She was torn between wanting to fling her arms around his neck and hiding in the coat closet. "I can see that," she replied, lowering her own guard to let him see her misery. "It's just me."

"No, it's me." He shifted his hold to stroke her collarbone with his thumb. "It's knowing that after we clean up here, before I do leave, I'm going to want to kiss you, and you're not sure you can trust me to stop at that."

Her heart pounding in her ears, she shook her head. "You're wrong. I wouldn't have brought you here if I didn't trust you."

For a moment he looked as though he might forget about the dishes. She could see it in her eyes. They bored into hers, and his skin seemed to be stretching more tightly over his high cheekbones. Even the nostrils of his arrow-straight nose flared, as though he couldn't capture enough of her essence. For a subtle, unconscious gesture, it was overwhelmingly sexy. Several times tonight, as she'd met his gaze, there had been these same undercurrents stirring between them, secret messages, unanswerable questions. Desire. When he'd dropped his eyes to her mouth, as he did now, she'd been glad her dress had a black background and a bold print; at least it didn't provide a blatant advertisement of her body's sensual reactions.

But just as she sensed he was going to give in to impulse, he released her and went back to filling the basin. "You'd better put the milk back into the refrigerator," he suggested with unbelievable aplomb. And with that he squeezed some liquid detergent into the filling basin.

Erin did as he instructed only because she was too dazed to think for herself. The rest—down to replacing the silk plant arrangement in the center of the table—she achieved by rote.

"You're slipping on your end of the deal."

Embarrassed at being caught daydreaming, Erin spun around and saw that he'd already filled the dish drainer with plates and glasses and had no room left to set the freshly rinsed bowls. "You are fast," she muttered, snatching up a clean towel.

"I never advertise what I can't deliver, Slim."

Erin tried to think of an appropriate retort, but nothing came to mind. Tongue-tied at thirty-two, she thought with disgust. She was in worse shape than she'd imagined.

She worked as quickly and quietly as he did, and they finished in minutes—or else the minute hand on the stove clock melted from all those burning glances she'd shot it. After he'd rinsed the last pot, she directed him to throw the pan of water out back, explaining it was less wasteful than pouring it down the drain. While he was doing that, she put away those things that belonged in the hardest-to-reach places. When she got to the mixing bowls, she turned around and lifted herself up onto the counter to reach the top shelf.

"Female ingenuity," Navarrone said, returning. Setting the dishpan back in the sink, he helped push the bowls to the back of the cabinet. "I don't think this needs to stay on, do you?"

Without waiting for a reply, he shut off the stove light, casting the room into darkness. Near darkness, he amended, his eyes adjusting to the soft, amber radiance filtering in through the screens from the porch light. It cast a glow that was magical, and made the woman before him surreal and more desirable than ever.

"I really do appreciate the help," she murmured, seemingly as fascinated by the play of light on his face as he was with the play of light on hers.

Struggling to find the words to share his own thoughts, he took the towel from her and set it aside. The brief contact allowed him to discover how cold she was. Nerves. She was suffering from a worse case of nerves than he was. "And I," he murmured, lifting those chilled hands to his lips, "really appreciate you saving my sanity tonight."

"Did I?"

He placed them on his shoulders. "You know you did."

"Don't give me too much credit. I was only hoping."

"And now?"

"Now I'm wishing we'd have that first kiss behind us."

"Slim...there's no reason to be nervous, and why would you want to wish away something that special?"

"It might not be special for you."

God, he wanted to hold her, soothe her, love away all those bad memories. He settled for brushing her hair behind her shoulders. "It's going to be wildfire, lady. Feel the heat building? We won't have another moment like this one again. Yeah, there's a little fear . . . but a lot more anticipation. Then you'll know what it's like to have my mouth against yours, and the mystery will be over."

"You make it sound almost sad."

He brushed his thumb across her lower lip, saw it tremble at his touch and felt longing churn inside him. "In a way it is. It's also a moment to cherish and respect, because it leads to other things far better than mystery."

"This is the second time you've surprised me with profound, beautiful words." Her faint smile held bemusement. "It's a startling contrast to the image."

"The gun I wear is part of the job, and the boots and jeans happen to fit this kind of environment. But that doesn't mean I'm rough edged through and through."

"No, you're very sensitive and patient. It seems—" she averted her gaze "—I'm the one who's become rough edged. I'm worried I might disappoint you, Navarrone."

Tenderness and violence made strange companions as they ricocheted through him. As he framed her face with his hands, he prayed for ten minutes with the bastards who'd destroyed her confidence and spontaneity. "How the hell are you going to do that?" he rasped, edging closer until his lips hovered before hers. "I'm aroused just from talking to you. All I ask is that you be honest with me, Slim, and then you can't possibly disappoint me."

Knowing he'd stretched the moment beyond reason, feeling his mouth was as dry as the air in a drought and that his stomach was screaming for a release of the tension clawing at it, he touched his lips to hers. Finally. No more nerves, no more space, there was nothing but the moment.

He'd fantasized about this. Reality, he discovered, was much more vivid. Soft and pliable, she inched closer and followed his lead like an enraptured student, first matching his brushing caress, then strengthening the kiss when he did, to more of a rocking motion. Her lips were like warm satin, their flavor—he needed to find out and lightly drew her upper lip between both of his—lush and intoxicating. Hungry to taste it again, he opened his eyes to seek her lower lip and discovered that hers were open, as well; they'd probably been open all along.

"Slim, you're going to go cross-eyed if you keep watching me like that."

"I don't want to forget this is you."

Her words sliced through him like a jagged knife. "It's me," he reassured her, his throat as raw as when he'd sat alone the night after he'd buried his mother and wept for the loss of both his parents. "Touch me." He shifted her hands to his face. "See? No one else."

She could have been a sculptor the way her long-fingered, unpampered hands explored him. Cheeks, brow, mustache, jaw, she indulged herself in a slow, sensual exploration that left him having second thoughts about how much of this seductive torture he could bear to invite.

"You're burning up."

To ease some of the yearning, he nibbled on her lip again. "I should be. I've been wanting this, wanting *you* from the beginning."

"Maybe it's all happening too quickly."

"Slim," he growled with gentle teasing, anxious to erase the doubt from her voice once and for all. "We're not exactly setting new speed records. One kiss in practically a month does not a scandal make."

She dropped her gaze to his mouth. "In that case, maybe we could . . . improve the ratio?"

Had he ever met a woman more unaware of her power? The instant she offered him her lips again, Navarrone knew if she ever healed to where she regained her appreciation of her beauty and desirability, she would bring him down like dynamite reducing a mountainside into beach sand. Hunger for more, for everything she had to give, surged through him so absolutely that when she parted her lips to catch her breath, he couldn't resist taking advantage.

A breathy moan rose from deep in her throat. She flexed and tightened her fingers against his chest like a cat testing its claws. Her heady tastes intoxicated him, and he caressed her, teased her and coaxed her into tangling her tongue with his. The throb of rising passion wasn't unfamiliar to him, but never had it possessed this sharp edge of desperation. In fact, this whole impulse to lose himself in a woman's softness was new, terrifying, yet unbelievably right.

She drew him closer, but he found himself coming up against her knees. For a moment, he forgot the restraint he'd committed himself to. Need and desire surged mindlessly into intent and he gripped her thighs to part them. But her instant stiffening snapped him back to reality with blinding speed.

"I'm sorry... I'm sorry," he muttered, self-loathing giving his voice a harshness that even he wasn't used to hearing.

"No, it was me. I shouldn't have closed my eyes, that's all."

"Why did you?" he asked, hearing something in that admission that had his blood thickening again.

"Because what you were doing felt so good."

It was what he'd hoped he would hear, what he needed her to say. The kiss he awarded to each corner of her mouth affirmed that with near reverence. "I have to get closer to you."

"Maybe if you'd . . . tell me. Tell me how much."

"How much closer I want to get, or how much I want to get closer?"

Erin groaned. "I can't believe you're able to joke about this. I thought we were going to be honest."

"You want honesty? Listen up." Holding her gaze, he eased himself between her legs. "I want to hold you so much I ache, and that's just the beginning. I want to experience it all with you. I want us to make love until we're so exhausted we can't move. I want to fall asleep, still deep and throbbing inside you. I want to awake from a dream that you're riding me and discover it's really happening. Just sitting across the table from you tonight, watching you touch your lips to a glass, close your teeth around a bite of steak and lick salad dressing from your lips almost made me climax."

The whole time he spoke, he inched closer until his chest came into full contact with hers. She wasn't wearing a bra, and the feel of nothing but two scraps of thin cotton separating him from her pebbly hard nipples was shades of heaven and hell.

"One day soon you'll trust me enough to let me see you. I'll undo these," he whispered, easing a hand between them to trace the path of the buttons down her dress. "Then I'll cherish you with my hands, warm you with my mouth."

"Navarrone, I'm the doctor, remember? It's not nudity that bothers me."

"What are you saying?" he demanded, wanting it spelled out. This was one woman with whom he would not risk making another mistake. There had already been too many.

"It's intimacy," she explained, her voice low yet clear. "The idea of lowering my defenses, taking risks. I haven't wanted that. But since I've met you . . . I dream about us making love, too."

He had to kiss her again and did, deeply, passionately almost before she'd finished her confession. She was quicksilver in his arms, and he couldn't get enough of her.

When he brushed his knuckles up alongside the outer swell of her breasts, her body's delicate tremor was as arousing to him as her lithe shape. After a second caress, he shifted to run his thumbs across her nipples. Their tautness and her muffled whimper told him what he'd already guessed—she was aching from suppressed need as much as he was.

She was by no means ready to give him all he wanted from her, but he knew he could ease at least a portion of her ache. But if he set her on her feet, he doubted her legs would hold her beyond the first seconds of the loving he wanted to share with her.

Breaking their kiss, he directed, "Hold me. Tighter."

Without giving her time to ask how or why, he slid his hands under her hips and swept her from the counter. It was only two steps to the dinette table. There he pulled out one of the chairs, sat down and settled her astride his lap.

His action didn't come without risk; for the first time she was able to feel the full impact of his arousal. "Too much?"

She released her breath slowly and shook her head.

Needing to touch her softness again, he covered her breasts with his hands. "Too fast?"

Instead of answering, she reached down to the first button on her dress and released it. Then another...and another, until she reached the tie at her waist. Her eyes, never wider or more mesmerizing, were hardly as confident as he knew she was trying to appear. Still, she held his gaze as she eased the dress off her shoulders.

The sight of her took his breath away. He'd known she was small, but his imagination underestimated how perfect. Her skin was creamy, her nipples the color of wildflower honey, tilting upward as though begging for his mouth. Drawn, as a starving man would be to the sweetest offering, he bent his head to her.

"Oh . . . please," she whispered, arching toward him for more.

"Unbutton my shirt. Let me feel you against me."

She did as he asked, though he didn't make it easy for her because he stayed close, intrigued with exploring her other breast. All the while his blood pumped and heated, threatening to sear him from the inside out. And then she had his shirt open. Unable to wait a moment longer, he pressed her to him, locked his mouth to hers and kissed her with all the emotions battling within him.

Had anything ever felt this perfect? Had anyone ever brought him this high this fast? Desire was a siren with Erin's face. With the same powerful need, he arched his hips and rocked her against him. Heaven and hell, he thought again. Too much and yet not enough.

His groan echoed his pleasure and his despair. Crushing her against him, he forced them both to be still.

"Navarrone?"

"Give me a second," he muttered, burying his face against the side of her neck, which was as hot and damp as every bit of his own body.

She exhaled shakily and stroked his back. "This isn't fair to you."

"Tell me you're not in any pain right now," he warned, only half joking, "and I'm going to—"

"Yes, I hurt. My breasts are throbbing, and here..." She shifted her hips ever so slightly, but it was enough to drag a groaned oath from him. "Sorry."

"Don't play with fire, Slim," he growled.

"I could get off you."

"Sure you could—but try and see how far you get."

She kissed his cheek and he felt her smile. It helped. So did her hands, gently massaging the tension from his shoulders.

"Navarrone...can I tell you something?"

"As long as it has nothing to do with sex."

"I'm serious."

Feeling as though every bit of his anatomy was being redesigned by a bulldozer was serious, too. "Go ahead."

"I only wanted to say that no man has ever made me feel what you have just now."

His heart, his very being, went still. He wanted to believe her, but heaven help him, he'd been too long the realist. "You were engaged," he pointed out, to remind her as much as himself.

"Yes, and Paul was special. But we were better friends than lovers. That's a terrible thing to say, only it's true. It was never like this."

He shut his eyes. "You are sheer quicksand to my good intentions."

"I don't under—"

"Come here," he growled, already cupping her head and claiming her mouth. One last time, and he would get out of there and go home to his empty bed. God help him, this relationship would be handled right. He'd wait—for as long as it took. He'd wait.

But in spite of his honorable intentions, he was miserable when he finally stood and drew her toward the door. "Walk me to my truck," he said, determined to bear anything if it meant spending a last few moments with her. The phone rang the moment they stepped outside. Resentment flaring, Navarrone wanted to pull the thing out of the wall.

Erin told him she had to answer it, or else her grandfather would come downstairs to find out why she hadn't. Watching through the screen as she picked up the receiver, he knew she was right. Besides, it could be an emergency. He smiled wryly, thinking how much more awkward—not to mention ill timed—the call could have been. But his smile vanished when he heard her say the caller's name.

Griff.

He met Erin's pensive gaze through the wire mesh. *Hang up,* he wanted to demand. *You're mine now. Mine.* But he wanted *her* to make that decision, and so he waited and listened to the one-sided conversation, his body still throbbing with the need to find fulfillment in hers.

She didn't hang up—not for what felt like ages, and with each comment she made, his blood began to pulsate in his veins because of a different kind of passion. Hurt. Pain. Indignation.

Finally she came back outside. He stared at her, absorbing the picture she made with the amber light turning her skin to satin, and he felt the most primal urge to throw back his head and roar with the fury of a wild beast.

But this was Erin, who'd once before come too close to the beast that lurked inside men. That knowledge had him gazing up at the star-bright sky and tempering his base instincts. "Tell me you didn't do what I think you did," Navarrone said heavily. "Tell me you didn't just accept Keegan's invitation to their Fourth of July picnic?"

"Excuse me?"

"Hell and damnation, you did. Well, you can forget it. You're not going."

She stared at him. "No one tells me what I can or can't do, Navarrone, and to be accurate, I haven't agreed to anything. What's more, whatever Marsh Keegan is or whatever he's done, his son remains my friend. I have every right to see him if I choose."

"I must be losing my mind," he muttered, beginning to turn away. Then he swung back and pointed inside. "What

just happened in there? Between us? Did you mean anything that you said to me?''

"How can you ask that?" Erin cried, looking aghast. She
reached up to touch his cheek. "I meant every word. But
one doesn't have anything to do with the other. I initially
turned down his invitation. You must have heard me."

"I'd rather forget that display of conviction."

"The problem is that the insurance company that under-
writes the event, especially the fireworks display, has strict
policy requirements. Griff said one of the contingencies is
that there has to be a doctor present in case of an accident.
Believe me, after what you told me tonight, I don't relish the
thought of having to face Marsh anytime soon, but that
doesn't mean I'll turn my back on a friend. *If* I go, and
that's a big if, it will be for that reason alone."

Still, Navarrone shook his head. "I could understand just
about anything else, but I can't handle this." Afraid to say
more, he headed for his truck. Erin followed.

"You're punishing me because I don't look at things the
same way you do."

"Punish? We're both a little too old to act like children,
Erin."

"Well, what do you think seeing everything in black and
white represents? I won't condemn Griff for his father's
sins, Navarrone. My God—he could be your half brother.
How can you reject him this way?''

"The same way he rejected me. Through Marsh."

In the silence that fell between them, a coyote cried in the
distance and an owl responded in its own tongue. Like us,
Navarrone thought, hating the thought of parting from Erin
on such a note.

"Please," she entreated, "don't go away angry."

He had his door open. Abruptly he slammed it and pulled
her into his arms for a fierce deep kiss that she was soon

answering with equally reckless passion. *Oh, God*, he prayed, thinking dying couldn't hurt more, *please...please*.

"Slim," he finally muttered, rocking his forehead against hers, "I'm beat, I'm frustrated and I want you so bad my teeth ache. Don't ask me to drive away from you smiling, okay?"

Not trusting himself to say anything more, he climbed into his truck, and without so much as a parting look, he drove away.

How, he wondered, upon reaching his driveway—though he had no recollection of how he'd gotten there—how could his life get any more complicated than it already was?

Seven

———

"**D**o you realize it's past eleven? I was getting ready to send out the search parties."

Erin summoned a smile and apologized to Griff as they walked through the foyer to the living room. Inwardly, however, she had to admit she'd been wondering whether she would make it here herself.

Every day since his call for help had been a trial for her. Things were getting progressively busier at the clinic, and the shipments from Claude Simpson meant working longer hours to log items and find a place for them. Teresa was a great help and so was Gramps, but he'd decided to use the cozy environment to hold a one-man colloquium on Navarrone's admirable qualities—as if she needed convincing. Worse, the day before yesterday, she and Navarrone had had their most heated argument about the Keegan's party. She hadn't been able to make him understand her ability to separate providing medical care—for what in effect would be many of her own townspeople—from what Marsh Keegan had done or may be guilty of. He saw it only as a division of loyalty: her choosing her friendship with Griff over her feelings for him. They hadn't spoken since, and the emotional impact was more devastating than she could have imagined.

"I had no idea the parking situation for this gala had turned into such a challenge. I was beginning to wonder if I was going to have to walk from the front gate," she said, hoping the observation would help offset additional questions about her tardiness. She didn't want to have to lie, but she couldn't be truthful and admit she'd been postponing her arrival, either. "You don't mind the official look, do you?" she added, glancing down at the white doctor's jacket she wore over her aqua-green jumpsuit. So far, the fashions she'd noticed ranged from silk sundresses to walking shorts, from business suits to jeans. "I thought since I'm here in an official capacity, I should wear something that would make me stand out in the crowd."

"You would do that no matter what you were wearing," Griff replied smoothly.

"I wasn't hunting for a compliment."

"Why not? I was about to myself."

Chuckling, she considered his white-striped shirt, tan dress jeans and matching boots—attire that may have been bought off the rack, but at a very expensive store. "You won't lack feminine attention today. How's that?"

"A bit light on evocative adjectives, but we can work on them later," he replied, giving her an intimate smile as he hugged her to his side.

Two men sat on the far side of the room, their heads together for what looked to be a business deal in the making. A few more people wandered by, admiring the sculpture that was as plentiful and valuable as any in an Albuquerque gal-

lery. A ferret-faced woman with a photographer in tow eyed
Erin and Griff speculatively. Erin stifled a groan. All she
needed was to be cornered by a columnist with a bent toward writing creative fiction. It was bad enough that the
county paper would be doing its usual two-page spread on
this event.

"Um, where's your father?" she asked, fingering her
loose topknot. She wasn't looking forward to having to face
Marsh, but it might be easier than dealing with a society reporter.

"He's holding court out on the patio." Griff stopped her
by a painted armoire. "Let's put your medical bag here.
This way it won't be a hassle, but you'll know where to find
it if you need it."

Afterward, he led her to the mezzanine with its opened
French doors. With every step up the stairs, the noise level
increased. Country-and-western music competed with
laughter and the steady buzz of multiple conversations until Erin felt as though she were entering a giant beehive. The
heterogeneous variety of scents were the second-greatest
assault on her senses: barbecue smoke, freshly cut grass,
flowers and enough samplings of women's perfumes and
men's colognes to stock a cosmetic counter.

Stepping out under the covered back deck, they paused to
view the sprawling scene. Even though her parents threw
some sizable parties of their own, and she'd seen enough
festivals in her travels to fill a tourist guidebook, Erin
couldn't deny the Keegans had outdone themselves this year.

Directly before them was the huge patio, encased by a
rock garden, where she immediately spotted Marsh Keegan
dressed all in white. He resembled something between a
character out of a Tennessee Williams play and a Latin
American dictator. His wheelchair was strategically placed
beneath an umbrella-covered table to protect him from the

already blazing sun. Several other affluent-looking people sat with him—clones, Erin decided drolly, from one of her mother's favorite type of soirees.

Beyond them in the gazebo, the band slid professionally into another song. There was a drummer, two guitarists, a fiddler, a stunning redhead at the synthesizer and a lead singer, who was busy connecting his electric banjo to the amplifiers. It struck Erin that she could have kept track of the Keegans' success over the years through the progressively larger size of their bands alone.

To the right of the gazebo, the lawn spread to an Olympic-size pool packed with screaming children and teenagers flirtatiously eyeing other teenagers. Up on the deck chairs, lotion-covered sun worshipers sprawled between more sensible shade seekers, grouped beneath colorful fringed umbrellas.

On the left side of the gazebo was a truly energetic group, fiercely enjoying a volleyball tournament. Beyond them were the tennis courts, where the nets were being removed for the dance that would follow the evening fireworks display.

"Brings back memories, doesn't it?" Griff said, leaning so close his breath tickled her ear.

Indeed, she thought. In years past she had enjoyed all this. Those had been innocent years, even happy ones, but thinking about them now made her feel sad rather than nostalgic.

"There's more people than ever," she said, groping for something to say. Silently, however, she wondered at the growing realization that many of the faces were unknown to her. Where were all the Azul people she'd expected to see in droves? This was the one day when the Silver Edge Ranch was literally an open house to anyone who wanted to stop by. Could it be that she'd underestimated the number of people who shared Navarrone's opinion of the Keegans?

"Here's the bar," Griff said, coaxing her toward one of three set up around the area. "Why don't we get something to drink before I take you to see Dad?"

Erin declined, which didn't stop Griff from ordering himself a double bourbon. Considering the hour, that disturbed Erin.

"Well, I see she finally made it."

Marsh's gruff acknowledgment rose above the surrounding clamor. With a sigh, which Erin couldn't help but note, Griff led her down the cemented incline to the patio. Though she nodded politely to the other guests, Erin had to steel herself against showing her revulsion when Marsh's narrow-eyed gaze skimmed over her body. But then the corners of his mouth twitched.... She stared, and was grateful for her control.

It couldn't be! she thought. She was simply falling victim to the power of suggestion—or had Navarrone smiled in that same sardonic way? Were their mouths similarly shaped? Were their eyebrows both bold and set low over their eyes?

Stop it, she ordered herself, taking a calming breath. A thousand other people shared those characteristics. Anyway, it didn't matter; Navarrone might brood over what blood ran in his veins, but it didn't, wouldn't, change how she felt about him.

"How are you, Mr. Keegan?" she asked, her tone neutral.

"Just dandy, Dr. Hayes. Couldn't be better, except maybe if Don here was to tell me he could buy me another fifty years," he rasped, waving his ever handy unlit cigar in the direction of the distinguished but bored-looking man beside him.

"You'll probably be around long after I'm gone, Marsh," the salt-and-pepper-haired specialist told him.

Marsh looked amenable to the idea. "Dr. Donald Carstairs, Dr. Erin Hayes."

Erin exchanged civil but reserved greetings with the physician. It wouldn't be fair to say she didn't like him, but she didn't condone empty encouragement. No wonder Marsh was pleased with his new doctor. The man was telling him exactly what he wanted to hear and probably charging an outrageous fee in the process.

"Everything looks most impressive," she told her host, for once grateful for the countless lectures on etiquette and diplomacy her mother had drilled into her.

"It should. It's costing me enough."

Then again, she'd never been one to conform entirely. Unable to resist, Erin drawled, "Well, you know what they say. One good turn deserves another."

Marsh's shrewd eyes glinted like polished steel reflecting the sun. "You're developing into quite a wit, young lady."

Under the pretense of wanting to introduce her to other friends, Griff quickly drew her away. On the other side of the buffet tables, he stopped. "What on earth was that for?"

His handsome, youthful face showed his distress, but, upset herself, Erin replied, "The thing I dislike more than being patronized is being treated as though I were an insect under a microscope, Griff. I'm afraid your father manages to achieve both with me."

"Honey, it's just his way. It always has been, only you weren't around enough to notice. Try to understand. You'll get used to it."

"Have you?" she asked, grateful he'd opened the door to this topic. It was past time for this conversation. "I'm beginning to notice he treats you even worse. He didn't say a word to you while we stood there. As far as he's concerned, you're the insect that's already been analyzed, classified and—'' She closed her eyes, knowing she'd pushed too hard, too soon. "Oh, Griff."

His laugh was mirthless. "Hey, you're right," he muttered, viewing the ice he was swirling around in the bourbon. "I've been analyzed, classified and summarily dismissed. And do you know as what? Average. I'm a simple, average guy who happens to have made the unfortunate mistake of being fathered by a man who requires someone more dynamic, intelligent and...aggressive for his heir. My curse for taking after the wrong parent." With a shrug, he lifted his glass to his lips.

Wishing she'd kept her mouth shut, Erin tried to ease the pain he hid with sarcasm. "That was my bad mood talking. I know he loves you."

"He wants to. That's not the same thing. He *wanted* to love my mother, only he couldn't. It finally drove her away."

"I didn't know that." Erin was beginning to wish she'd asked him more questions when they were younger. "I'd just assumed that she'd died, like his first wife."

"She might as well have, since I never heard from her again. That's the trick, you see. He'll tolerate anything but desertion. Leave and you're exiled permanently."

"It still hurts, doesn't it? Her abandoning you, I mean."

"Nope. What hurts is that I'm beginning to hate him as much as she did in the end. Damn it, *I* stayed. I deserve more than his 'good intentions.'" He took another drink and then gave a brief, hard laugh. "What do you think of that confession, Doctor? Scary stuff, huh?"

During the past few days, while she'd been reviewing all that was unfolding around her, Erin thought about how she would handle this conversation. She'd accepted that it was inevitable. But she'd never imagined it would occur at a moment like this, when they stood amid a few hundred people on a day that was supposed to celebrate freedom, hope and the fruition of dreams.

"Let's walk over by the horses," Erin suggested, looping her arm through his. "I need to be able to hear myself think."

On the far side of the house, well away from the revelry, about a dozen horses stood in the roomy pen. Since it was a holiday, most of the hands had the day off and, as a result, so did their mounts. As Erin and Griff approached, a black-maned chestnut trotted closer. The rest continued to either feed or drink from their troughs.

"I wish I'd thought to bring you a carrot from the buffet table," Erin told the curious horse. She stroked its powerful gleaming neck before turning back to Griff. "Do you think you can be happy continuing to live here?"

"What kind of question is that? I was born here. This is home."

She shrugged. "I was born in California, and though I enjoy periodic visits, I don't consider it home. That's what I'm trying to say. Sometimes your needs, your dreams, take you away from your roots and make you start new ones elsewhere. So I suppose what I'm asking is, are you where you want to be? Is ranching fulfilling your needs?"

"Not all my needs," he replied, his gaze roaming over her face in a way that made Erin wish she could rephrase the question. "But all this is going to be mine someday. I'd be in a lot of trouble if I didn't love it."

"And how does your father fit into your scenario?"

"There's the question of the decade." Sunlight glinted in Griff's hair as he glanced up to consider the near-cloudless sky. "I guess I want him to be more of a friend and less of an authoritarian. Hell, I'm thirty-three years old, Erin. I should be making more decisions around here than whether to buy feed on a Monday or a Wednesday and garbage like that. I know how to run this place as well as he does. I have ideas that would improve our efficiency and cut expenses. But he refuses to give them a chance. He refuses to pass on the reins of control or even share them."

"I think part of that is because he's very aware of his mortality, Griff," she said, trying to be fair. "He knows his time is running out, and he's hanging on."

"I'm trying to take some of the load off him, so he *can*."

Erin nodded in sympathy, having recognized as much herself. Textbooks were full of case studies and theories about the relationship between fathers and sons. It would take more than a five-minute pep talk from her to help Griff with his monumental plight. "I wish I had some easy answers for you."

"I know." He drew a deep breath and brushed away a wisp of hair that had been blowing against her cheek. "Just talking to you makes me feel better, though. You've always had a gift for making people believe they're worthwhile."

"Good grief, you *are* worthwhile."

"Yeah, well . . . I know I haven't said this enough, but I cherish your friendship, Erin. The letters you always sent for Christmas and the funny cards you managed to find for my birthday . . . they meant a lot."

Enough to allow her to pose a question that would test that friendship? "Griff, I need to talk to you about something else."

"That sounds serious."

"It is. In fact, I'd be too embarrassed even to bring it up if you hadn't said what you did just now."

"In that case, fire away. The last thing I want is for you to be troubled by anything. Especially if it has to do with me."

"Even if it has to do with the shootings going on in the area?"

His sun-bronzed face paled, then flushed—with temper or embarrassment, Erin couldn't tell which. But otherwise, there was no physical change in his demeanor. For a moment she wondered if he was going to answer her at all. She wouldn't blame him if he didn't. A good friend wouldn't doubt. A decent friend would have more faith. It was only when she saw his white-knuckled grip on his glass that she realized what was building within him.

"So," he replied flatly. "Santee's gotten to you, as well."

Erin closed her eyes. "Please, hear me out. I'm not doubting *you*. It's your father. Not Marsh himself, of course, but..." She shook her head, disgusted that she wasn't making sense even to herself. "I wouldn't blame you if you decided never to speak to me again, but I have to ask this. There are serious accusations being made, and I'm concerned for your sake."

"Accusations by Navarrone Santee. Don't deny it, Erin," he muttered, his eyes acquiring the same hard glitter of complete control his father possessed. "I'm only sorry you don't realize he's using you to get to me. He's wrong about Dad. My father may not be a saint, but he's not that cold-blooded, either. I swear to you, I would know if he was authorizing something so terrible. No, Dad's not involved with the shootings."

She'd never seen him look so earnest or so distant, and never had she felt so torn. "I've hurt you deeply."

"Yes, you have. I wonder...do you even have a clue that I'm in love with you, Erin?"

She stood there for several seconds, thinking she was doing well to breathe. And as for thinking of something to say...

"You're surprised. But pleasantly, I hope. You also need time to sort out your loyalties. I can understand that, as well—and I'll be patient."

It was the second time this week that the term "loyalties" had come up, and it, along with Griff's confession, had Erin's heart feeling like a ship taking on water from all sides. "Griff... I don't know what to say."

"The truth needs no words." Planting a kiss on the tip of her nose, he slid his arm around her waist and turned her back toward the house. "Stop looking so forlorn. Everything's going to work out. Now come on, we have a party to enjoy."

Enjoy turned out to be the overstatement of the week. By the time the sun had gone down and people were grabbing lawn chairs and spreading blankets in anticipation for the fireworks show, Erin was exhausted.

After Griff's declaration, she'd walked around in a blur for what seemed like hours. Sometime during the day, she'd ministered to a child who'd fallen by the pool and scraped his chin and elbow raw. She'd also treated two people for heat exhaustion. In between, she'd managed to get through dinner at the Keegan table, somehow achieving small talk with the governor, the mayor and various businesspeople. But now her head was throbbing and the barbecued shrimp she'd only nibbled on didn't seem to want to settle in her stomach.

It was possible she might have gotten a touch too much sun herself. Aware she had to last through the fireworks, Erin went inside and took two aspirins from her bag. Needing something to take them with, she glanced around. She didn't want to go back outside quite yet; just the thought of being cornered by yet another person in search of free medical advice for some overdramatized symptom made the headache worse. She chose to head for one of the bathrooms, instead.

As she crossed the foyer, someone called out. Her name? Unsure, she detoured into the study.

Marsh Keegan sat in his wheelchair in the middle of the room, looking as though he'd been waiting for her all along. Why not? she thought. After all, he'd only been staring holes into her most of the day.

She steeled herself. "Yes, sir?"

"Sir! My, how you manage to hang on to your manners. Where were you off to just now?"

"A bathroom to take these," Erin replied, indicating the pills in her hand.

"Have we given you a headache, Dr. Hayes?"

"It's been a long day. You appear tired yourself."

"I am, actually. But I wanted to talk to Griff before I go upstairs. Where is he?"

"He said something about double-checking things with the fireworks crew. Would you like me to tell him you need him, once he gets back?"

"What about Caulfield? Where's he?"

The mere mention of the man brought an unpleasant taste to her mouth. "I have no idea. I haven't seen him for hours."

Marsh fell silent, and she decided to use the moment to excuse herself, but as she was about to, he drawled, "You don't like me, do you?"

Headache or not, this was a challenge she couldn't ignore. "I used to think I wanted to. At least, understand you."

"But I've made the prospect so unattractive, eh? I guessed as much," he muttered, adding more energetically, "Well, don't think I'm about to apologize. This is a hard world, young lady. To hold your ground you have to be tougher than everyone else."

"Isn't it interesting that most of the people who've shared that view have been dictators?"

Her host's laugh was brief and harsh. "Dictators, diplomats . . . do you want to know the difference? Knowing how to exert just the right amount of pressure to get what you want. Control, that's the secret." He looked up at his portrait and sighed. "I may not have achieved everything I aspired to do in this life, but I never lost control."

Erin's dinner made a dangerous lurch for escape. How dare he, she thought, nearly pulverizing the tablets in her hand.

Some of her feelings must have showed in her expression because Marsh Keegan's face turned amused. "You've got spunk and you've got class, I'll give you that. But you've also got too many foolish ideas in your head. I told Griff that sleeping with a woman he couldn't control would be like keeping company with a rattlesnake. He's not listening, though. You're what he wants."

"Is that supposed to be a compliment?"

"I don't give compliments, I state facts. My boy's bent on having you. You use some sense for a change and accept him when he pops the question. I'd like to hear the sounds of life continuing in this house before I'm done."

Good Lord, Erin thought. To think she'd once thought him merely outspoken. "I'm not a brood mare, Mr. Keegan. And as much as I care for him, I'm not in love with Griff."

"Love." The old man snorted. "Love's another one of those fairy tales the world would be better off without. I'm not saying a woman should enjoy herself in bed less than a man, but there's no reason to muddy up things with foolish gibberish. Human nature is human nature."

"Is that how you justified your behavior to Anna Estevez?" Erin lashed back, her fury bubbling over.

Marsh Keegan's head shot up, his eyes impaling her. "That gossip was dealt with over thirty-five years ago and has no place in this house."

"Thirty-seven to be precise. Quite a legacy for the woman you raped to pass on to her son."

The blood drained from his face, leaving it ashen. "Get out. Get out of my house and take your lies with you," he croaked. "Raped . . . I never raped Anna. She was mine, do you hear me? Anna was mine!"

Erin took a step backward and then another. She couldn't believe what she was hearing. His? The man was twisted. Fighting another wave of nausea, she spun around and bolted from the room.

All she could think of was getting out. The house was suffocating her. The very idea of sharing the same air he breathed was a repugnance she could no longer tolerate. Running back to the living room, not caring who saw her or what they thought, she retrieved her bag from the armoire. Nothing mattered except putting distance between herself and this place. She thought of her obligation to Griff to stay, but knew that was now impossible. There were at least two other doctors on the premises. Maybe they weren't general practitioners, but she wasn't about to split hairs. Right now it was her sanity that had to take priority.

She ran all the way to her car, passing early departees who wanted to get away before the mass exodus began. They eyed her with curiosity, but she didn't care. She didn't care about the falling temperatures, either. Feverish, she stripped off her jacket and, after unlocking the driver's side, tossed it and her bag inside.

The station wagon protested against her rough handling. It coughed and lurched when she pushed too hard on the accelerator; it squealed as she spun out the front gate and onto the road back to town; it grunted and groaned over every hole and bump she blindly steered into. Erin hardly noticed any of it, not even the fireworks that began illuminating the sky to her left. She was too angry, too shocked, too ill.

How could she have been so blind, so stupid as to not see all Marsh Keegan was before this? *Oh, Navarrone.*

A coyote shot out of the darkness and dashed across the road. Erin hit her brakes, fighting the car as it skidded and nearly slid off the road. She winced at the beating the tires took on the uneven ground. All she needed was a flat tire. She was miles from anything, including a phone. More careful, she got the car back on smoother ground.

She'd driven a minute or two farther when she spotted the lights of a vehicle approaching from the range on the left. Just after it crossed the cattle guard and before it turned onto the road, Erin's lights showed that it was a dark gray pickup truck—with the silver Keegan brand on the passenger door. Then the truck's lights blinded her.

She shielded her eyes from the brightness. When the vehicles were side by side, however, she glanced over to try to see who was in the cab.

The driver was a man, but he wore a cowboy hat low over his eyes. It would have been impossible for her to identify him—except, Erin realized with a jolt, that she knew that hat. Rather, she'd seen its uniquely rolled brim before.

What in the world was he doing out there? The dirt road was barely more than two tire tracks leading up into the mountains. It was so rough only dirt-bike enthusiasts, nature lovers or treasure hunters would risk testing its drivability. It wasn't any of her business, of course. Not really. Unless . . .

She took her foot off the accelerator and glanced in the rearview mirror. The truck's taillights were out of sight. Without giving herself time to reconsider, Erin made a U-turn and headed back toward the turnoff.

The dirt track was worse than she'd imagined. Though she was driving at a turtle's pace, the car's front end still hit a low spot and scraped the ground. Another one or two of those, she warned herself, slowing even more, and she would definitely spend the night out here.

Way off on her left she could see the star bursts of red, green and gold over the Silver Edge. But barely. She was closing in on the mountains, was already in a moderate climb and beginning to round a bend.

Everything outside the beam of her headlights was black. Spooky. It was a childish word to think of, but she was feeling more vulnerable by the minute, and crazy. Certifiable. If Navarrone was angry at her before, he would be furious with her when he heard about this. Maybe she wouldn't tell him. It was bad enough that he was angry with her for having gone to the party; there was no sense in volunteering a confession about this wild-goose chase.

Thinking of him was comforting, though. Reassuring. So was discovering that her hunch about the truck was wrong. There was nothing out here. What she had to do now was find a relatively smooth place to turn around and— She gasped and simultaneously hit the brakes as a wild-eyed creature dashed through the beams of the station wagon's headlights. It reappeared farther ahead, and this second glimpse allowed her to identify it as a horse, a baby horse.

She shifted into park. "Oh, don't run away," she entreated, fumbling for the glove compartment where her grandfather kept a flashlight.

The rush of adrenaline that hadn't quite receded after her confrontation with Marsh pumped with the renewed force of a runaway freight train. Thrusting open the car door, she heard the young horse's cries of distress above the car's idling engine. It was a sound that tore at her heart.

The colt, or filly—she had no idea of its sex—kept rushing back and forth, frantic, its immature voice slicing into the night like the most terrible of nightmares. Erin battled with dread and her desire to help. The last time she'd heard such cries, she'd spent the night caring for the wounded and burying the dead, all the while trying to deal with her own terror. She wanted nothing more than to get away from that memory and this place. Instead, she rounded the back of the car to avoid the car's headlights and used her flashlight to find her way into the darkness.

"Easy, sweetheart," she called soothingly to the animal, who kept darting off. "Show me where to go. Easy..."

She literally stumbled over the first victim. There wasn't time to do more than gasp. As she hit ground, the flashlight slammed hard and went out.

Don't you dare get sick, she ordered herself, pushing back onto her knees. She took a deep breath, then another and another. In all the years she'd practiced, she'd never thrown up, not even in med school. She wasn't going to start now. But her hands shook as she wiped them against her thigh and then fiddled with the flashlight. When the light came back on, she pointed the beam on the abnormally still creature before her.

Tears filling her eyes, she ran her hand along the animal's still-warm body, first out of grief and then to seek a pulse. She swore at herself because she wasn't as quick to locate the key spots on a four-legged creature. She compressed her lips against a sob when her fingers came in contact with its wounds, but she found no pulse.

She moved on to the next and the next, all the while continuing to croon to the baby. She didn't know if it helped the horse. It kept her from losing control.

The fourth animal was not only breathing, it weakly tried to lift its head when she approached. Excited, Erin ran back to the station wagon for her bag and anything else she could think of that might be useful. So preoccupied with her hunt, so intent on listening to the foal's neighs above the car engine, she was completely unprepared for the sound of her name and a hand on her back.

Erin screamed. She came out of the car with only one intention: to protect herself no matter what the cost. She would not be this monster's next victim. But she'd struck only one blow against the hard wall of a man's chest before being completely and inescapably trapped by powerful arms.

"Easy, Slim," his urgent voice ground out against her ear. "It's me. It's me!"

She'd realized as much the moment her face was crushed to his chest and she'd breathed in his unique masculine scent. "Thank God!" she cried, reaching up and wrapping her arms around his neck. "I thought he'd come back. I was so scared."

"You little fool," Navarrone groaned, holding her equally tightly. "You're damned lucky it was me. Hell, you're shaking all over and chilled to the bone. Come sit in my truck. I'll turn on the heat and we can talk there."

"No." Immediately her thoughts went back to the job at hand. "I have to help." She tried to reach back into her car for her things, but his hold on her was unyielding. "One's still alive, Navarrone. Let me go."

"Erin, you're in shock."

"Let me go, damn it!" Somehow she jerked free, grabbed her things and ran. Navarrone caught up with her a moment later, having retrieved a stronger flashlight from his own truck.

"Sweet Jesus," he breathed when his light illuminated the scene.

"I think this is its mother," Erin said, nodding to the foal that was edging closer. "If you'll keep your light like that, I'll have both hands free to work. If I can—"

"Slim, it's no good," Navarrone said, taking a more gentle hold of her arm. "There's only one thing left to be done. Come on. I'll take you to my truck. I have to radio to the station for someone to phone Kyle Langtry and the game warden."

Erin fought him like a woman possessed. Suddenly she was no longer under the dark New Mexico sky. She was once again in a foreign land, fighting hands that kept her from Paul and the others. "Stop it! I can help. Oh, please, I have to try to help!"

But Navarrone's greater strength prevailed. He lifted her as though she weighed no more than a child. Ignoring her threats and the curses she flung at him, he carried her away.

Eight

"**W**here are we? Why did you bring me here?"

Navarrone shut off the station wagon's engine and turned to Erin. He'd thought she was asleep, or at least pretending to be. She hadn't said more than a dozen words since he'd put the foal's mother out of her misery, nor had Kyle or the others' arrival prompted a change in her reticence. She'd withdrawn to her own car and spoke only when spoken to, her tone as listless and empty as the expression that had settled in her eyes.

She was scaring the hell out of him, and he wasn't sure how to reach her, let alone help. He had a multitude of questions, too, but so far he hadn't been able to bring himself to ask more than the most necessary, such as what had compelled her to go out there, and could she identify the vehicle she'd mentioned? Neither of her responses satisfied him. A woman driving home at night didn't turn down a desolate road simply out of whimsy, not even a woman as brave or crazy as Erin. Especially when she claimed she couldn't describe the truck that had intrigued her.

"This is my home," he said, reaching over to retrieve one of the pins slipping from her topknot. Her hairdo was falling, her face was smudged and her clothes were a mess, but he'd never wanted or needed to touch her more. "You were in no shape to drive, so I asked Kyle to have someone bring back my truck later."

She confiscated the hairpin. "Why didn't you take me home?"

"I would if I thought you'd wake Wil so he could sit with you."

"I don't need anyone to sit with me."

"And I say you do. You're a knot of nerves, Erin." When she didn't argue the point, he continued, "All I want is for you to come inside for a while. Wash up. Maybe have something to drink. After that I'll take you home."

He could almost hear gears turning as she considered his suggestion. Then, abruptly, she got out of the car.

Navarrone followed, holding his sigh of relief until he was outside, where it merged with the mildest of breezes. He glanced at the sky. It was the kind of night for stargazing; this evening the glittering points of light appeared particularly close, within an eagle's reach. Under different circumstances, he would have come home, done his chores and, afterward, cleansed his mind and soul by sitting on the steps, basking in the utter magnitude of it all. Tonight he would stay earthbound.

He returned his gaze to Erin only to discover she'd stopped and was staring at his corral. Inside was the baby horse that had been captured only a short while ago. "That's why I ordered the trailer. When you saw the game warden's people drive away with her, I told them I'd take her until we can find a good home for her," he said.

"Her?" Erin murmured. "A filly. She...she has to be terrified being all alone in there."

"A little. It can't be helped. I haven't had any livestock for a while." A few months ago, after he lost his dog, a longtime pet, he'd needed a break from getting too close to anything or being responsible for another living creature. He'd even sold the few dozen head of cattle he'd owned.

"What kind of people do such horrible things?" she asked in a voice he barely recognized. It was higher than usual, reedy, almost childlike.

The question forced him back to the present. "Selfish people. Unconscionable people. The frightening thing is that their power over the rest of society is spreading. You'd think it would be easy enough to track them down—someone has to know something, heard or seen something. But people are afraid. They know that those who take the law into their own hands don't stop there—they intimidate and bully. If witnesses aren't concerned for themselves, they worry for their families. Until we can convince them that they'll be protected, or until the guilty make a mistake we can catch them at, the carnage will continue."

Erin rubbed her bare arms. "I'm cold."

Navarrone wanted to pick her up and carry her inside, she looked that unsteady and fragile. But aware of how receptive she would be to the idea, he touched his hand to her back and directed her toward the side door. He'd lived in the two-bedroom house since he'd been a boy. In daylight it showed its age and modesty, but he'd kept it painted and neat. Neither he nor his parents had been fancy people. They'd preferred living away from town, and his nearest neighbor was still more than two miles away.

Inside, the house wasn't much fancier. The fluorescent light he turned on pointed that out. As Navarrone led Erin through the stark white-and-black kitchen to the cozier but hardly stylish living room, he tried to see the place through her eyes. Even though he'd come to know she wasn't a person to put a lot of value in material things, he found himself suddenly wishing he had more than there was.

"What can I get you?" he asked, bordering on a case of awkwardness he hadn't felt in years.

"Could I . . . ? I need to wash."

He led her to the bathroom, turned on the light and indicated where the clean towels were. "Feel free to hunt around for anything else you need. I'll be outside seeing to our little friend," he told her before closing the door behind him.

It was fifteen minutes or so before he returned. He could hear the splash of water coming from the bathroom, and it made him wish he could strip and step under the brisk shower spray himself. Right, he countered in the next instant. Who was he kidding? It wasn't the shower that appealed to him; he wanted to be with Erin, and he wanted *his* hands to be the ones spreading soap over her body.

After washing up in the kitchen sink, he got himself a beer from the refrigerator. The loud sound of the tab made him realize the bath water had stopped running. She would be coming out soon and expect him to take her home. Heaven help him, that was going to be tougher than bearing her silence. He wasn't ready to let her out of his sight yet.

He'd almost snapped once he'd realized it had been the station wagon he'd spotted and followed. The thought of what she could have walked into, that—like Fred—she could have ended up at the county coroner's even now had him nearly polishing off the rest of the beer. How could he let her go without sharing those feelings with her?

A sound—more like a shift of the air—caught his attention. He turned and lowered the can to the counter.

"I couldn't find a bathrobe."

"I don't own one," he replied, feeling as though his voice belonged to someone else.

With a faint nod, she returned to the task of rolling up the sleeves on his pale blue shirt. "I had to rinse the blood out of my jumpsuit and I'm letting it dry a bit. This is from your closet. I hope you don't mind?"

"Of course not."

He couldn't look at her enough. The shirt was sizes too large. It reached her thighs, modest by anyone's standards, except on someone with legs like hers. Wet, her hair was a dark brown mantle. Droplets of moisture dripped from it, doing their best to soak the shirt and causing the material to cling to her in places that played further havoc with his imagination.

Though he'd never seen her with much makeup, her freshly scrubbed face made her look vulnerable. But nothing drew him more than her eyes. They were shadowed with fatigue, mirroring an anguish he wasn't sure he could reach if she would let him try. Desperately wanting a chance, he took a step toward her. "Are you ready for that drink now?"

"No. I don't think it would stay in my stomach. But..."

"Yes?"

"Hold me?"

She didn't have to ask twice. Another stride had him before her, enfolding her against his pounding heart. Only, he'd been wrong to think the shower had helped. She was still trembling, which extinguished some of his relief and pleasure.

"What is it?" he asked, tilting his head in order to see the face she pressed to his shoulder. "What are you wrestling with?"

"You. Me. Everything."

He wasn't certain what to make of that. Was he even on her wavelength? All he could do was guess, be here for her and hope his body didn't embarrass them both. "We're on no timetable, Slim. I thought you understood that from the other day."

"I don't know what I understand anymore, or believe," she muttered, before leaning back to gaze up at him. "Make love to me."

He couldn't have been more surprised if she'd asked him to walk into the shower fully dressed. She was in no emotional condition for what she'd just asked, did she think he didn't see that? Yet at the same time, it told him how far tonight's tragedy had pushed her. She was at her threshold, which was only compounding the nightmare still troubling her.

Navarrone framed her face with his hands. "Do you know how badly I want to do that? But tonight I had a ringside glimpse of what it would be like to lose you. It cut past bone, baby. I don't think tonight's a night I could stop if you suddenly realized you'd asked for too much."

"I won't ask you to stop."

"Erin."

She touched his lower lip. "It's what I want."

Then heaven help them both, because he wanted it, too. Maneuvering to escape her coaxing fingertips, he closed his mouth over hers.

His kiss was deep and, though still restrained, showed her a glimpse of what she was inviting. He had to give her one last chance, he thought, reaching for the severing threads of his willpower. But instead of going stiff in his arms or retreating from the hot thrust of his tongue, she offered her own with a surprising boldness that sheared those threads of restraint like a razor slicing through cobwebs.

He anticipated the whimpering sound she made as he abandoned the last of his resistance and kissed her with the full force of his desire. Whatever else he expected, though, it wasn't the eager burying of her fingers deep into his hair, signaling her acceptance—more—that she couldn't get close enough to him. As a result, it was he who was left shaking like a tin shed in a gale.

Nothing had ever felt so good yet hurt so bad. Impulses as old as time and as basic as breathing tempted him to draw her with him to the floor here, now, to sheathe himself in her, to possess her. But as he opened his eyes out of need and wonder, and saw surrender in her own gaze, he knew he couldn't take her as a conquest. She was a gift. A gift he was beginning to understand only too well.

Without thinking what it might cost her, she meant to push him beyond reason. She wanted him to take all control and choice away from her. Her motive—to win herself a fast trip to oblivion. Lifting her into his arms, Navarrone decided they would both reach that destination, but they would make the journey his way and at his own pace.

His bedroom was cast in shadows from the light angling in past the half-closed bathroom door. A narrow beam hit the white wall and diffused to illuminate his bed. Hot-blooded by nature, he usually slept with only a top sheet, if even that, and the one he lowered her onto was as stark in its simplicity as it was in its whiteness. No fancy extras, he thought again, with another spasm of regret. Then the sight of her with her wet hair fanned out and spreading a damp halo, his shirt riding tormentingly higher on her thighs, had his regret following the path of his noble intentions.

Stretching himself out by her side, he kissed her again, but slowly this time, dragging a throaty, sensual moan from her that sent his heart and his temperature soaring. With a deliberateness that soon made her breathing grow shallow, he unbuttoned her shirt. Fingers splayed wide, he slid his hands inside, over her shoulders and down her back, drawing the shirt with him. The movement lifted her from the bed and she let her head drop back, exposing the vulnerable arch of her throat. Drawn to it, he ran his lips down its elegant length, reveling in the discovery of creamy textures, seductive scents of soap and woman, finally lingering where her pulse fluttered like a fretting bird.

The constriction of her shirt-entangled arms disturbed her. She began fighting it, first in frustration, then with growing panic. "Navarrone... help me."

"Easy, Slim. Shh," he soothed, his words barely more than a rough whisper, while in short order he freed her. "See? It's gone. Concentrate on me." As he spoke, he moved downward, using his breath and especially his hands to caress her. A man spent his entire life taking his hands for granted, but directing his ten fingertips on a languid discovery of the shallow rises and hollows of her lithe body, Navarrone knew he wouldn't commit such an oversight again. Never again. "Concentrate on this," he murmured, retracing his journey to her right breast. He blew lightly around the pale outer curve, a full circle that he repeated using his index finger, then again with his lips. With each completion of a circuit, he narrowed his course until he came to the sensitive peak, taut and beaded in anticipation and yearning.

She writhed beneath him, toward him, asking with her body what he knew she couldn't yet ask with words. Knowing exactly what she needed, he lowered his mouth to her and took them both to the next plateau of pleasure.

Her deep-throated moan excited him, and wanting to hear it again, he performed the same ministrations on her left breast. When he felt her fingers begin fumbling with his shirt snaps, he made short order of the task by grasping a handful of material and jerking. Snaps popped and cloth ripped.

Her surprised, smoky laugh was as sexy as it was too brief. Navarrone thought nothing could arouse him more, until he watched her rapt concentration as she pushed his shirt from his shoulders and visually worshiped him. Having anticipated a long wait to see such desire light her eyes made him realize he'd guessed wrong. There was no limit to how high she could take him. Needing her hands on him, he directed them to his pounding heart, pressed them closer and locked his mouth to hers for another mind-drugging kiss.

Soon, praying she was ready for more, he eased his fingers under elastic and simple cotton—cool mint-green cotton—he amended, remembering the glimpse he'd had when he first lowered her onto the bed. But there was nothing cool about the womanly secrets his exploring fingers discovered. He worried she might freeze up on him, and she did go still, but it lasted only a second, and then she was opening to him, trusting him, letting him.

She was so hot…so tight…so sleek…he shuddered, the wild beat of his heart challenging his determination to make this good for her. But he couldn't resist the need to see her. She felt like paradise. After he slid that last scrap of cloth down her long limbs, he knew he could easily spend the rest of his life gazing at her and showing her how beautiful she was to him.

Her hands, however, were indulging in a lesson of their own. The third time he failed to escape their attack on his belt buckle, he gave up, rose and stripped off the rest of his things.

Dangerously vulnerable now, he felt sensations coursing through him like wildfire wherever she touched him. He loved the bite of her fingers tangling in his chest hair, and her method of disclosing what parts of him intrigued her most. Again and again she returned to explore favorite areas until his nipples ached, the rigid plane of his belly felt like molten lead, and the hairs covering his thighs—sweet salvation, he thought with a groan. From the waist down he was at attention, all but pleading for another complete inspection.

His entire body throbbing, Navarrone guided her hand to his thick, rigid length. When her exquisitely capable hands closed around him, he thought he would die of pleasure. Knowing he was close, he moved against her and sought her eyes to see what he would read there. If he saw any hesitation, any doubt whatsoever, he knew it might indeed kill him, but he would stop. He worried unnecessarily, however; her gaze reflected only trust and breathtaking desire.

"It has to be now," he rasped against her lips, already shifting as his throbbing heat sought the center of hers.

She smiled, though shakily, and his heart exploded, love pouring through him even as he slid into her. "Too heavy?" he rasped, trying to brace the bulk of his weight on his forearms.

She swallowed. "No."

And pigs flew, he thought, swearing silently as he watched tension build within her. "I'm hurting you," he groaned, torn between concern and his own pleasure that was threatening to overtake him even before he felt her body's slow acceptance of his invasion.

"Yes—no. I mean ... *Navarrone.*" Abruptly, maybe involuntarily, she shifted her legs to draw him even closer and exhaled with a shuddering moan. "I can't ... I can't believe I'm already this close."

A droplet of sweat streaking down his face fell onto her lips. Before he could swoop down and lick it away, she greedily captured it with her tongue.

He didn't know what got to him faster—her honesty, her responsiveness to him or her wanting everything, anything, he had to give. Groaning because the end was only heartbeats away, he framed her face with his hands and watched her as he withdrew and repeated the entry that had won him that confession. Then he did it again, and again. Heat, white hot, mingled with wild need. Never had he experienced a more intense craving for release; the power of it pulsated in his brain until he thought he would explode.

With the last crumbs of his sanity, he lowered his head until his lips brushed against hers. "Come with me," he whispered. And, locking his mouth on hers, he drove them both over the edge.

Erin couldn't stop trembling, couldn't catch her breath and couldn't hold Navarrone tightly enough. Though they were swiftly diminishing to shadows of what she'd initially felt, spasms continued to shoot through her body like courseless rockets. She wanted to cry, to laugh, to share with him everything that was in her heart. Opening her eyes, she met the gaze of the man who'd given her back her life.

His breathing wasn't much steadier than hers. Each time they happened to inhale in unison, their passion-dampened bodies came in contact for a most unique variety of kiss. It still amazed her that someone so big and powerful could show such restraint and tenderness. Even now, as he tried to ease to her side, there was a renewal of hunger darkening his bottomless eyes.

"Don't leave me yet," she murmured, tightening her arms.

"I'm crushing you."

"You feel wonderful."

The breath he exhaled sounded like a sigh of relief. "No bad moments?"

"No. And you didn't hurt me, so please don't worry, because I can see that's where this is leading." She reached up to brush his hair back from his forehead. Dear heaven, she thought with new awe, he was magnificent. Her body turned liquid and her heart ached just looking at him.

He leaned into the caress like a big cat wanting petting. "You're getting to read me pretty well," he murmured, his voice rumbling like distant thunder. "What am I going to do when there's no mystery left?"

"That'll be the day." She flicked a hand to the numerous bookcases lining two walls of the room, which were crammed full of hard covers and paperbacks. "You should have seen my face when I came in here to raid your closet. This is a small library you've collected here. I don't know what's intriguing me more so far—the pathology books or the collection of William Stafford poems, and I've only had time to browse through the first few shelves."

"I told you. When a man's resigned himself to the fact that he's going to spend a lot of nights alone, he'd better think of a good way to pass that time. I got my degree through mostly correspondence courses," he added more soberly. "But the one year I did actually attend college, I had the luck to fall into the hands of an iconoclastic scholar whose inability to toe academia's political lines had reduced him to seeking tenure at my junior college. God knows what he saw in me, but with wit and a damned smooth bottle of Scotch he lured me into a deeper appreciation for the world inside books."

Erin had no trouble understanding what had drawn the man to Navarrone. He was a diamond in the rough, part saint and part demon. A very human man who made no pretenses about being anything but what he was. An analytical man who struggled with a lot of life's questions. She wished she could have met his teacher to thank him for his insight.

"To think I didn't want to like you," she murmured, exhausted by simply thinking of the emotional distance they'd traveled to reach this point.

"And now?"

Reality turned with a vengeance, bringing with it a pain that centered like an ache in her throat. "Now I'm afraid I'm going to hurt you."

"What makes you think you will?" Navarrone asked, his wariness apparent, even though he pretended to be fascinated with the taste of each of her fingers.

How could she answer that without telling him what she'd seen tonight? She needed time—not because she wanted to keep anything from him, but because by sharing what she knew, she would have accepted her obligation to give legal testimony—legal testimony that would inevitably hurt a friend. She needed to come to terms with that herself. What could a few hours hurt?

"I hate to see you in conflict with yourself," he added when she failed to answer him. "But I respect you too much to push. Just know I'm here for you. When you think the time is right to tell me what's wrong, I'll listen."

Erin closed her eyes. She'd hurt him. She could see it in his gaze and hear it in his voice, and it reminded her of what a tenuous line she was walking. If she wasn't careful, if she didn't resolve things in her own mind soon, she could destroy these wondrous feelings growing between them. "Maybe I should be getting home," she murmured, shifting slightly to give him the subtlest of hints.

"No."

"My grandfather will be worrying about me."

"No, he won't. While you were showering and I was outside seeing to the filly, Kyle brought my truck. I asked him to stop by your place to let Wil know what happened and that you were with me."

Erin groaned. "You realize, of course, he's going to jump to conclusions?"

"Not incorrectly."

"He'll be incorrigible."

"We'll get used to it."

We. The word, as well as seeing intent flickering again in his eyes, made her tremble with anticipation. In response, Navarrone drew a deep breath and, slipping his hand beneath her head, lifted her toward him for another deep kiss.

"Stay with me tonight," he demanded finally, burying his face against the side of her neck. "I know I'm being greedy. You've had a long, lousy day but . . . damn it, Erin, I need you."

Gripping his hair, Erin forced him to raise his head, and she searched his face to see for herself. People had said they needed her before—in fact, for most of her life. It came with the territory when you were classified as sensible, practical and dependable to a fault. Even well-meaning Paul had offered need as a basis for justifying their engagement. But no one had ever said, "I need you," to her with the gut-wrenching emotion Navarrone just had. Men who spoke *that* way to a woman did so for only one reason. Oh, Lord, she thought. She wasn't strong enough to resist such temptation, but the danger she was flirting with . . .

"Then I'll stay," she told him, drawing him to her. "We'll leave the world outside for a few more hours, and give to each other. Tenderness . . . passion . . ." *Love,* her heart whispered, seeing the truth as clearly in his eyes as if she were reading a printed declaration.

Afraid he might speak the word, Erin pressed her lips to his. She couldn't bear to hear all that was in his heart yet, not when she knew he might regret the words later. All she would accept for now was another few hours in his Eden, where her only challenge was to squeeze a lifetime of loving into one night and where the only enemy was dawn.

"Do you know how I've dreamed of you coming to me like this—" he skimmed his hands down her body and cupped her hips "—without fear, without doubts, wanting me as much as I want you?"

Erin matched the intense rocking motion of his hips with her own. One night, she assured herself, if they could have this one perfect night, she would find the strength to deal with everything else.

Summoning confidence in her sensuality, which was easy to find when she was in his arms, Erin gently urged Navarrone on his back and followed to tease his lips with hers. "I do want you."

And to show him how much, she sat up so she was straddling his masculinely beautiful body. Tossing her hair behind her shoulders, she gazed down at the mesmerized expression on his face and smiled.

"Do I look more confident than I feel?" she asked.

"I don't want you to do anything you don't want to," he replied, though already his hands were moving over her in physical worship.

"And I want to please you—as much as you've pleased me."

"Slim, you could lie here like a slab of granite and I'd die a happy man just looking at you."

Laughter and sex—she'd never considered the possibility. But she had a feeling that with Navarrone possibilities were limitless. Leaning forward, she stroked her breasts against him, until her nipples ached and his skin turned feverish. She gave him long, lush kisses until his pulse pounded at his temples and his own mouth bit hungrily at hers. She took his hands and, sitting up, showed him where she needed to be touched, stroked.

He had fantasies and she wanted to be the source of all of them tonight. He'd already given her so much. Never had she felt so alive, so adored, so safe—and all by this man whose face now appeared carved from stone, a study of tension and raw hunger.

Navarrone. His name was a whisper in her heart as she began the ride he craved. Never taking his eyes off him, meeting his burning gaze with a smile that had his rough hands gripping her softer body with tender ferocity, she gave herself up to a sensuality she'd never before dared.

Soon he joined his movements to match hers, and their ride was unhurried, though intense, as intense as their hands when he laced his with hers. She wanted to prolong the moment, but knew it couldn't last. Already ecstasy was shooting through her like flame-tipped arrows. His heat was impaling her, reaching deep, reaching all the way to her soul.

Navarrone.

He was the essence of the very air she sucked into her lungs. When he drew her down into his arms and crushed her to him, the spasms that were beginning to claim her were equal to those racking his body.

''Navarrone!'' she cried again and again.

All he answered was a brief, guttural yes. And that, she decided later, was as it should have been, for his was the name of rapture and, finally, peace.

Nine

He couldn't remember falling asleep, but when next Navarrone opened his eyes, he saw the hint of daylight at the edges of the curtained windows—and Erin, resting her head on her elbow watching him. Immediately, memories of last night flooded his mind and stirred his body. Last night she had been brave and vulnerable and sweet. This morning, with her tousled hair and her eyes full of mystery and secrets, she made him think of a Gypsy. He reached up to wind a silken strand around his finger, grateful that they still had a while before they had to let reality—not to mention their respective jobs—intrude.

"Have you been doing that all night?" he asked, breaking into a lazy smile.

Though slumberous, her shrug still did dangerous things to the sheet she'd tucked demurely above her breasts. "Sleep's always been overrated, anyway."

"Come to any conclusions?"

"A few."

"I hope at least one of them is X-rated."

Erin's soft laugh became a yelp when he scooped her up, rolled her over him and onto her back on the other side of the bed. In the process she lost the sheet. As he gazed at the delectable picture she made—despite the shadows under her eyes that contradicted the validity of her previous statement—Navarrone felt the strongest urge to keep her in his arms and hold fast. It didn't seem possible that anything this good could last, he thought with a flash of fear. After all, what in his life ever had?

"I could make you coffee and breakfast while you shower," Erin suggested, interrupting his brooding. She tested his morning beard with the back of her fingers.

"Or we could do both together."

He watched some troubling thought cast a cloud over the light in her eyes, momentarily turning them a storm-threatened forest green. As quickly as it had come, however, it passed, and the hint of a smile tugged at the corners of her mouth.

"Are you always this insatiable?"

"There aren't any notches on this headboard, Slim," he replied, fast losing interest with tiptoeing on eggshells. When a man wore a size-twelve boot, he soon learned there were some things he wasn't going to be good at. "I'll admit I've never liked sleeping alone, but sex has never been an all-consuming preoccupation with me. What appeals to me is the idea of having someone of my own to love and understand, who'll love and understand me back." As soon as he heard himself admit that, however, he grimaced. "That sounds like a bunch of manure, doesn't it?"

"What it sounds like is that you're going to miss out on all the hot water."

She was off the bed and dashing for the bathroom before he could react, a beguiling flash of bouncing hair and enticing curves. With stomach muscles clenching in a way that had nothing to do with any desire for food, Navarrone kicked off the rest of the sheet and followed. By the time he sated this hunger consuming him, she was going to call him the biggest fraud she'd ever met.

Steam was already rising from the shower stall, which had been one of the improvements he'd made that his father had never gotten around to. Opening the frosted door, he stepped inside, oblivious to the hot spray stinging his body.

Erin had wrapped a towel around her head turban-style to protect her hair. As he took the soap and washcloth from her hands, he wondered if she would still be wearing it when they finally shut off the water.

"That's my job," he told her—and proceeded to drop both items to the floor.

An incredulous laugh burst from her lips, followed by a gasp as he wrapped his arms around her and tugged her completely against him. There wasn't even room for the beads of water sluicing down their bodies. "I thought—"

"Entirely too much," he growled, exploring the sensitive spot near her ear he'd discovered last night. "How sore are you?"

"I'm not," she replied, equally preoccupied with massaging the muscles on his arms and chest. "I told you, you've been very gentle with me."

"Maybe not this time." He could feel her rising excitement in the tremor that raced through her body. Following the water's path down her back, he let his hands relish the tempting curve of her hips, the sleek firmness of her thighs and the heat simmering between them. "This time I want you to let down all those guards. This time I want you to introduce me to the woman no one else has even glimpsed."

"You don't ask for much, do you?"

The irony in her voice had him smiling inwardly. She was so confident as a professional, but she still had no idea of her power as a woman and his lover. "What do you want to bet I can make you wet and weak-kneed by just talking to you?" he murmured, bending to discover what tap water tasted like on her breasts.

"You're not just—" Her voice broke as he not only tormented her with his tongue, but with fingers that slid beyond silky curls to the sensitive flesh he'd explored again and again last night.

"Talking?" Already hard and aching to be inside her, Navarrone repeated the caress. "Yeah, well, there's talking and then there's . . . talking."

"Navarrone."

"So hot. You're hotter than last night, and I thought then that you were going to go up in flames." He sucked sweet air into his lungs as she shifted her hips, seeking more of him. "Yes. Take me. Wrap your legs around me and . . . damn. Exactly like that."

She learned so quickly, and so well. With hands he was afraid were too eager not to bruise her, he gripped her hips and took what she offered, thrusting deep. He didn't try stifling the cry of ecstasy that ripped through him. Everything he was and everything he dreamed to be came excruciatingly, sharply, into focus, centering on the woman in his arms.

Love me. More. Please. They were her words—but had he been able to find his voice, they would have been his. Still he wanted, needed to say something. Only, ecstasy came like a tidal wave, lifting Erin toward her peak. Holding fast, he raced her over its crest and seconds later joined her for the equally thrilling ride down.

* * *

"Oh—you're ready. You take cream in your coffee, right?"

Navarrone paused in the doorway of the kitchen and, watching Erin replace the picture he kept on the lunch bar, finished closing the row of snaps on his clean white shirt. The photo was of his mother and father, and he didn't know why she was acting embarrassed at having been caught looking at it. Considering what they'd shared, had shared through the night, she had every right to look to her heart's content.

"A touch. It seems to agree with my stomach better that way."

"Do you have problems?"

"Only a little ulcer." The immediate concern on her face did more for him than a cabinet full of medicine. "It's no big deal, Slim."

"Excuse me? Who do you think you're talking to? There's no such thing as a 'little' ulcer. Furthermore, if I want to be concerned, I will be." She pushed the mug of coffee she'd just poured to the end of the counter and bent to look into a cabinet. "I don't know why I should be surprised you have one. You're only carrying the worries of the world on your shoulders."

"Look who's talking."

"Don't get smart. Where's your electric skillet?"

"I don't have one. There's a cast-iron pan one cabinet over." Rolling up his sleeves, Navarrone grinned. The idea of being "tough-loved" by Erin was as appealing as having her soft and willing. But his smile waned somewhat when he glanced back at the photo. "So what's your verdict about this?"

He was grateful she didn't intend to play coy. She set the pan on the stove and looked at the picture again. "I'm not sure. As I told you when we met, I see some Anglo in your features, but mostly you favor your mother. She was lovely," she added gently.

Navarrone considered the somber-faced woman whose coal-black hair had matched Erin's in length. "She was, and she had a soul that matched her beauty."

"What was your father like? You know, you're less open about discussing him."

"I suppose that's because I'm always wondering whether I have a true right to claim him or not. He was a rock," he said abruptly, feeling a rush of love and respect for the man with the piercing blue eyes and rawboned face. "Tough as they come, except around my mother. All she had to do was walk into a room and you could feel them gravitate toward each other.

"He died in a high-speed chase," he added quietly. "Lost control of his car and slid into a gas-station pump going seventy miles an hour. Helluva thing, considering how far apart the damned stations are around here."

Grateful Erin didn't offer any sympathy or comment, he took a sip of his coffee. "My mother never got over losing him. It didn't help that I was grown and in the service. Not long after I got out of boot camp, she became ill. The doctor said she needed an operation. I came home on leave and found her sitting in the rocking chair my father bought her one Christmas. She'd died holding that picture. It made me angry that I was cheated out of a chance to say goodbye. I lost it. Chopped up the chair and burned it stick by stick. You do stupid things like that when you're young, hoping they'll make you feel better. But there have been nights when it would have been good to have that chair to sit in."

He sighed, set down the mug and faced Erin. "Are you ready to talk to me yet?"

For a moment he thought she might possibly hedge this time, but then she simply turned off the flame beneath the pan. Rather than look at him, however, she stared at the bubbling margarine she'd just put in the pan. "I'm afraid."

"Of me?"

"For you. For what I know you'll do when you hear what I have to say. And, yes, *of* you. I'm afraid you're not going to forgive me for not telling you sooner."

Unable to stand this emotional and physical distance between them, Navarrone solved the latter problem by coming around the counter and taking her in his arms. "Slim, after what we've shared, you should know better than to believe that could happen now."

"I kept something from you last night," she said, not lifting her gaze from the badge he'd pinned on his left shirt pocket. "When I said I couldn't describe the truck."

He'd known—well, guessed really—that there was more than what she'd told him. "And?" he asked quietly, telling himself it would be all right.

"It was gray with the Keegan brand on the door."

"You saw the driver, too, didn't you?"

"No. Well, not clearly."

"Erin, this isn't the time—"

"He was wearing a hat low over his face. But it's the same kind of hat Van Caulfield wears. The same shape. When I was young, my grandfather told me that the way a cowboy wears his hat is as much a trademark as a brand is on cattle. The one I saw was rolled tightly to a sharp V, the way Van Caulfield wears his."

This was exactly the kind of break Navarrone had been waiting for, but rather than giving a whoop and spinning her around and around, he stepped away from her. Instead of being relieved and pleased to know that he finally had a viable witness to present to Kyle, he felt sick to his stomach.

"Aren't you going to say something?" Erin asked, unease making her voice unsteady.

Oh, yes, he could think of plenty. "Is that why you let me make love to you? Did you think that you could barter yourself to get mercy for the Keegans?"

"How can you even suggest that?"

"What the hell else am I supposed to believe?" he snapped back. "It's obvious you didn't trust me."

"I needed time to think!"

"*Think?* After what you witnessed last night?"

"Why is that so hard to understand, considering how you're reacting? I needed to resolve in my own mind whether I should go to Griff myself and tell him about Van, or risk you doing exactly what you're doing now. Don't you see?" she entreated, reaching for him. "You haven't even considered that Van Caulfield might be operating alone."

"Give me a break."

"There. That's exactly my point. You're convinced, so the Keegans are as good as tried and convicted. Well, that's not how I operate."

"How can you be so naive as to keep believing in their innocence?" he ground out, tempted to grab her and shake some sense into her.

"I didn't say they were innocent, and I'm not even talking about Marsh. In the last few weeks and especially after last night, I've seen a side of him that makes it clear he isn't the person I used to know."

"He never was. Wait a minute—what happened last night?" Navarrone demanded, unable to stifle his concern for her despite his fury.

"We had words, but it wouldn't serve any purpose to repeat them. But I will tell you that I had a conversation with Griff and I pointedly asked him about the shootings."

"Let me guess—his sincerity brought tears to your eyes."

"He assured me that he would know if something like that was going on," Erin replied, holding her head high.

"So what this amounts to is that you believe him and not me. That's great. That's simply—" Unable to restrain the violence and pain threatening to strangle him, Navarrone swept his mug off the counter. It flew across the room and crashed into the kitchen table, splashing coffee and pieces of the mug everywhere.

Silence hung like death in the room. Finally, stiffly, Erin moved toward the sink and reached for a dishrag.

"Leave it," Navarrone ordered. "It's my mess. I'll clean it up."

She froze and wrapped her arms around her waist. Dressed in her jumpsuit, which still bore some stains, Navarrone thought she looked no less devastated than when he'd found her last night. Unfortunately he was fresh out of the compassion he'd offered her then. He wasn't sure what he felt, but he knew he didn't trust himself to go near her.

"I've known him since we were children, Navarrone," she explained, staring at the spreading puddle on the floor. "No matter what Van Caulfield or Marsh has done, that has to account for something."

"Maybe. But should it count more than being honest with the man you've taken as your lover?" He left the room. When he returned he was wearing his holster and gun.

As he headed for the door, Erin ran to block his way. "Where are you going?"

"Call Kyle Langtry and tell him what you've told me, and tell him to get to the Silver Edge right away." He moved her out of the way as though she were a mannequin.

She grabbed his arms. "You can't do this. You have no warrant, and you . . . you'll be out of your jurisdiction!"

"This goes beyond jurisdiction and technicalities."

"Of course. Revenge always does."

Her words sliced straight to his heart, but Navarrone couldn't let it matter. Breaking her hold, he hit the screen door with his palm. It slapped the outside wall of the house before swinging back and slamming shut, but by then he was already out of its reach, and Erin's.

Erin didn't watch Navarrone drive away because she was already running to the phone. It took her three tries to dial Kyle Langtry's home number that was listed on the bulletin board by the phone. She had no idea how she was going to get the words out to tell him what was going on. Her throat was locked tight by the sobs she was fighting to hold back. As it was, she could barely breathe. Through the night while Navarrone had slept, she'd debated over what to do, how to tell him, how he would react, but she'd never anticipated it would turn out this way.

He'd left looking as though he despised her. And why not? She'd let him down. Her rationale didn't bear scrutiny, at least as far as he was concerned. She'd even failed at attempting to keep him from endangering himself.

It took a small eternity to reach Kyle Langtry. He was already out on the road, and they had to track him down and have him call her back. As soon as the phone began ringing, she scooped it up and rattled off her story, finding it easier if she opted for speed rather than coherence. Barely pausing for a breath, Kyle barked that he was on his way and hung up on her. Erin held no grudge against him for his rudeness. What was important was that he understood the magnitude of the situation. The sooner he was en route to the Silver Edge, the faster Navarrone would have the backup he needed.

Wondering if Navarrone had at least had the sense to call his own people, she dialed his office. Someone told her that he had indeed radioed in, but that he'd ordered them to stay put.

How could he? she thought, experiencing a new wave of panic. Wasn't there some sort of policy about going into sensitive situations alone, even if you were the boss? What if Van Caulfield tried something before Kyle and his people arrived? Erin demanded of the officer, who cleared his throat, mumbled and offered no reasonable reply. Furious, this time Erin was the one to hang up first, and with terror mounting, she ran to hunt down her keys.

The trip to the Silver Edge had never taken longer. Her distress grew when, upon arriving, she spotted Navarrone's truck, parked not at the house but by the stables, where a man sat on the tailgate of a pickup gingerly working his jaw. Erin pulled up beside him and jumped out of the car. "What happened?" she demanded, noticing the bruise that was already forming.

"Ain't exactly sure. I came outside and found Chief Santee in Caulfield's truck," he replied, jerking his thumb over his shoulder. "He was pulling out a rifle from behind the seat. I didn't think he should be taking it without Mr. Caulfield's permission, so I tried to stop him—only he sorta convinced me it wasn't none of my business."

"Where'd he go?" Erin demanded, looking toward the bunkhouses.

The man pointed in the opposite direction—to the main house.

Breaking into a run, she called over her shoulder, "Go put some ice on that bruise. It'll keep down the swelling."

Once at the front door, she went inside without bothering to knock. Immediately she heard raised voices. Following them to the study, she found Navarrone standing in the middle of the room before the ever-seated Marsh, who looked drawn and agitated this morning. Van Caulfield stood on the opposite side of Marsh's wheelchair, and Griff sat on the corner of his father's desk. It was he who saw her first.

At his look of surprise, Navarrone glanced over his shoulder at her. His scowl told her nothing had changed, at least not regarding his anger with her. "Go home, Erin."

"No." She was gratified to hear she sounded calmer than she felt. She eyed the rifle he held circumspectly—probably to protect possible fingerprints—in his right hand. Was that what he'd taken from Caulfield's truck? She knew nothing about guns, but it looked quite expensive and lethal. "Someone has to remain sensible about this," she added.

Following her glance, he set the rifle down against the nearest chair. "It's not loaded," Navarrone told her, only to rest his hand on the automatic at his hip, as though to remind everyone else that such was not the case with his own weapon. "We were just having a nice chat while we wait for the sheriff. Go on, Keegan," he encouraged the old man glaring up at him. "You were saying?"

"You go too far. I overlooked your behavior in the past, but—"

"Don't do me any favors."

"That's enough, Santee," Griff said coldly. "We don't know how you planted that gun, but you're not going to get away with this. Erin, honey, he's right about one thing. This is no place for you."

She stood her ground. "I have something to say, Griff. You should know that Navarrone's here because of me, because of what I saw on my way home last night." His only reaction was to take in her jumpsuit and draw in a deep breath. "I saw a truck a few miles down the road coming off one of those trails leading up to the mountains," she continued. "Something about it wasn't... It seemed odd that it should be there, so I turned around and followed the tire tracks up to the hills. There were horses, Griff. Dead horses."

"Damn. Sweetheart, I'm sorry."

He stretched his hand toward her in invitation. Erin watched as Navarrone looked from him to her and waited. She stayed put.

"I see that I was more accurate yesterday than I thought," Griff said, dropping his hand. "More's the pity. The important thing, however, is that you're all right. Do you realize the risk you took? What if someone had still been there?"

"I know. I wasn't unafraid, but please listen. What I haven't told you is that I was able to identify the truck."

Griff's gaze slid to his father and Caulfield. "Is that so?"

"And the driver." Wiping her damp palms against her thighs, she announced, "It was a Silver Edge truck, Griff... and your foreman was driving."

"The hell you say," Caulfield growled, taking a step forward. "I was here all night, and I have witnesses who will swear to it."

"Back off," Navarrone warned, pointing at him.

Griff scratched at his right sideburn and gave Erin a quizzical smile. "Are you sure it was Van? Couldn't it have been someone who maybe borrowed one of our vehicles? Considering the number of people we had out here, it would be feasible for anyone to do that. After all, we usually leave the keys in the trucks."

"I didn't see the man's face," Erin admitted, feeling the full weight of her accusation bearing down on her. "But I did see his hat."

"You're accusing a man of a serious crime on the basis of a hat?"

Griff's gently patronizing tone had her lifting her chin. "How many of your people wear one with the edges rolled quite the way his is?"

"Where *is* your hat, Caulfield?" Navarrone drawled.

The blond man shifted from foot to foot and looked decidedly uncomfortable. "In my cabin or my truck. Heck, I forget where I put it."

"Since when does a cowhand forget where he's left his hat?"

"Seems to me, we're making a big fuss over a few damned horses that no one's going to miss, anyway," Marsh Keegan injected, before his foreman could respond.

Erin was unable to contain her disbelief or anger. "How can you say that? They're living beings, beautiful and free."

"They're parasites, girl, and they take from those that need. I don't know of one rancher who, if he's speaking honestly, wouldn't admit he'll be glad to see the lot of them dealt with."

"You mean the way Indians were dealt with when the white man decided he wanted their lands?"

"If there's anything that drives me to drink, it's a bleeding-heart liberal," Marsh muttered, and turned his attention to Navarrone. "Surely you can't believe anyone besides you will take her accusations seriously."

"Yes, I do."

"For a few lousy horses?"

"For the horses and Fred Guy."

"Oh, now wait a minute," Van Caulfield said, waving his hands before him. "No one's sticking any murder charge on me."

"They will once the ballistics tests are run on this rifle," Navarrone replied. "You and I both know they'll match the bullet taken from Fred's body, and between that and the witness at Fred's shooting, plus Erin's testimony, the state's going to have all they need to lock you away, Caulfield."

"Don't worry, Van," Marsh assured him. "Griff will call our attorney. You'll never even go to trial."

Griff cleared his throat. "I don't know, Dad. If Erin believes it was Van she saw—"

"Are you nuts?" Caulfield shouted, the veins at the side of his neck bulging. "I told you, I'm not doing time for a crime I didn't commit."

"Hey, don't sweat it," Griff replied. "The judge'll probably just slap you with a fine. And I think Dad would agree with me that we'd be willing to cover that for you."

Erin couldn't believe what she was hearing. "How can you say that? The man's being accused of murder. I *saw* the carnage, Griff. Not all of those poor creatures died quickly. One of them left a foal!" she cried, her voice breaking. "Financially supporting Caulfield would be the same as condoning what he's done."

"He's been a dependable employee, Erin."

Van Caulfield swore. "Griff, you lousy... I'm warning you. I won't stand for this."

"Shut up!"

"No way, man," the foreman replied. "Keeping my mouth shut for you is one thing, but taking your rap is another." He bent over Marsh, resting his hands on the armrest and back of the wheelchair. "Mr. Keegan, if you can stomach what's being done to those animals, then you're going to be pleased as punch to learn the guy behind it is your own flesh and blood."

"Wha—Griff?" Marsh whispered.

"He's lying, Dad." Griff shifted farther back on the desk. "Cowards always start squealing when things get too sticky."

"Check the books more carefully, Mr. Keegan," Van said. "He's been paying me to scout for the horses, as well as to keep me quiet about what I know. He's hiding the expense as higher feed and supply costs. Then go to the Silver Mesa Gun Parlor in Albuquerque—a real class operation—and ask them if they remember the golden boy who came in a few months ago and paid cash for a .340 Weatherby Magnum along with enough ammunition to wipe out most of Azul, let alone a bunch of horses."

Like everyone, Erin was so caught up in Van Caulfield's announcement that she didn't notice Griff's movements until she heard the desk drawer slide open. Before she or anyone else could react, Griff was aiming an automatic at Navarrone.

"What the hell's come over you, boy?" Marsh exploded, pushing away Van and wheeling toward his son. "Put that thing down!"

Griff didn't take his eyes off Navarrone. "Sorry, Dad. I would have liked to handle this differently, but Van's forced me to accelerate my agenda. Santee, why don't you unbuckle your belt and ease it to the floor."

"In your dreams," Navarrone replied flatly.

Unable to believe this was happening, Erin stepped between the gun and Navarrone. "Don't," she whispered, facing the man she'd called friend.

"Erin."

She ignored Navarrone's harsh command. "Griff...think. What do you hope to achieve? I called the sheriff before coming here. He'll be arriving any minute. You can't possibly get away with this."

"She's right. And so far no one's been hurt," Marsh added, a beseeching note entering his voice. "We'll say it was a misunderstanding. For heaven's sake, don't do anything foolish!"

Griff's smile was bitter. "Thanks for the vote of confidence, Dad. I never have done anything right in your eyes, have I? Even now."

"Is that what this is all about?" his father asked, his expression incredulous.

"I've never been as smart as you wanted, as tough as you wanted. I wasn't anything like your *alleged* son." He grimaced at his father's shocked stare. "How could you think I didn't know? Hell, the whole town had been talking about it years before I was born! You want to hear what gives me the biggest laugh? You still don't know whether he's yours or not."

"Why didn't you tell me?" Marsh croaked.

"And then what? Would it have changed anything? No, I knew I had to prove myself to you. When you started bellyaching to the BLM boys about those damned horses multiplying like fleas in this area, it gave me the idea how to show you once and for all how important I was to you."

"Of course you're important to me, son."

"Bull. You can't see past your own ego and *him*," Griff spat, nodding toward Navarrone. "But it doesn't matter anymore, because you know what I learned in the process, *Father?* I'm as much of a bastard as you are."

"Griff." Erin stepped forward when she saw what his comments were doing to Marsh. The older man's face was turning an ash gray, and he was gripping the arms of his chair as though in pain. "Give me the gun."

He stared at her for a moment, his expression softening. But when she took another step toward him, he stiffened. "I sure don't want to have to hurt you, honey, so step aside."

Though she shook her head, Navarrone took hold of her upper arms and drew her backward. *"Do it,"* he rasped, placing her firmly behind him.

No sooner did he have her out of the line of fire than Griff corrected his aim.

Marsh uttered a strangled moan. "You can't!" he cried, hoisting himself up from his chair. He lunged for Griff's gun hand with a strength Erin knew any expert would have said wasn't possible for a man in his condition. Though his effort wasn't adequate to subdue his son, Navarrone's was. Wasting no time, he succeeded in wrenching the gun free, then knocked Griff off his feet with a vicious swing of the back of his hand.

Both father and son went down with a crash. Navarrone, wasting no time, quickly flipped Griff over and secured his wrists with handcuffs.

Erin hurried to Marsh's side. "Call Emergency and tell them to get a medical helicopter out here right away," she snapped at Van Caulfield, who had backed well away from the group as though distance alone could dissociate him from the others. Then she leaned over Marsh and started releasing his shirt buttons. "Try to relax. Keep breathing. That's it. I have to run out to my car and get my bag."

"N-no...too late."

"Hold on. We'll get you to a hospital."

"I want...I want to speak to Navarrone."

Erin glanced up to meet the gaze of the man she would have given her life to save. Though she couldn't tell what he was thinking from his closed expression, he crouched beside her.

"I'm here."

Marsh gazed up at him with glassy, haunted eyes. "You look so much like her," he managed between weak breaths.

Navarrone remained silent, but Erin could feel the tension emanating from him. She placed her hand on his shoulder, appealing for his tolerance just this once.

"Are you...? Quickly. Tell me...are you m-my son?"

"I don't know." He began to turn away, hesitated, then glanced back at the old man. "Be still now. Help is on the way."

Marsh Keegan closed his eyes. Moments later Erin felt the quiet exhalation that always seemed such an understatement to the finality of death.

Commotion struck again as Kyle Langtry and several men burst into the room. The sheriff took in the situation and shot Navarrone a you-couldn't-wait-could-you grimace. Without a backward glance at her or Marsh Keegan, Navarrone went to confer with his friend.

Ten

The sound of the screen door slamming behind him emphasized his house's emptiness to Navarrone. He'd left the Silver Edge as soon as he'd given Kyle a rundown of what had gone on. His friend had wanted to give him a good chewing out for breaking all the rules, but once he'd seen Marsh, there'd been an unspoken agreement to save it for another day. Navarrone was grateful; grateful, too, that Kyle said his office would be handling all the paperwork. Right now he wasn't in any shape to deal with reports. He wasn't even ready to deal with the mess he'd made in here earlier. All he could think about was Marsh Keegan's last words.

Are you my son?

For more than thirty years, despite the denials from his mother and the support from the man he'd called Father, the question had been the proverbial sword dangling over his head. No, not everything was resolved yet. But he knew a way it could be, once and for all.

He stepped over spilled coffee and broken shards of the mug that spoke of his earlier anger and frustration, and went to the back of the house. In the second bedroom, his old bedroom that was now a storage room, he headed straight for the closet and a four-drawer file cabinet. Crouching, he opened the bottom drawer and took out the firebox where he kept those few papers that weren't better off in a bank safe-deposit box. Beneath his insurance policies, his truck title and the medal his father had been awarded posthumously by the state police, he found the plain white envelope bearing his name written in his mother's neat hand.

Actually the envelope was no longer white; time and many hours of handling by him had caused it to yellow. The edges were bent and worn. The sealed back, however, was intact, just as when she'd secured it more than fifteen years ago.

Navarrone sat behind his desk and studied his mother's handwriting, as he'd often done when waging his private war over whether or not to look at what was inside. The lettering was small and even, the style light-handed—as much due to her growing weakness as her gentle touch—feminine yet precise. Anna Estevez Santee may never have graduated from high school, but she'd been proud of what skills she'd mastered.

Tearing the envelope open felt like an invasion. He wasn't surprised his hands were unsteady as he ripped the flap with his thumb. When he pulled out the single sheet of unlined paper inside, he smiled fleetingly at the painstaking effort his mother had taken to keep her writing in straight lines. She'd probably used up an entire tablet to get one copy where everything was to her satisfaction. That would be her way. Appearances had mattered with her. Pride counted. It was a lesson he'd never forgotten. Taking a deep breath, he read.

My Dearest,

I cannot help but wonder how long it will take you to open this. When you do, I only hope that you'll read with an open mind and an understanding heart, and that you will be able to forgive me for the times I was so rigid in my silence about the past. My excuse was that I was truly ashamed of what had happened to me. I thought refusing to discuss it would put it to rest, given enough time. But it hasn't really worked, has it? Despite my two lapses of silence when I denied those questions you posed to me, you have your suspicions, and your suspicions make you bitter.

And so it is past time I reassure you in the only way I know how, by taking pen to paper and swearing on the love I shared with your father that Marsh Keegan has no blood connection to you. You, my son, had already been conceived weeks before.

You've suffered much over this, even after those times when your father and I begged you to ignore the rumors and the tauntings. Still, I alone am to blame for your continued doubts. Because of my own relentless refusal to discuss Marsh or the past and my request to your father that he not speak of it, either, you could find no peace of mind.

But I believe there comes a time in every life when it is possible, no, necessary to release the ugliness in one's heart. When I look at the man you have become, my dear, I find that generosity. I must forgive Marsh Keegan his violation, for in a way it helped make you the strong yet sensitive man you are today. Even if you hadn't been the only child God decided I should bear, you would have remained my joy. Take strength in that, my love. Forgive Marsh Keegan and forget him. But above all, move on to find the happiness you so richly deserve.

Navarrone set the letter on his desk and, pinching the bridge of his nose, squeezed his eyes shut to ease the burning deep in their sockets. Fatigue left him drained and light-headed, as though he was emerging from a great battle fought totally in darkness. Neither his mind nor his body was having an easy time acclimatizing itself to peace and daylight.

Dropping his hand, he blinked, his vision blurred. It took him several seconds to realize Erin was standing in the doorway. She looked pale, and as exhausted as he felt—and more than a little unsure of herself. Not quite everything, he reminded himself, was resolved.

"What took you so long?" he asked, wondering if the rawness in his voice was as noticeable to her as it was to him.

"Kyle wanted to ask me a few questions." Her gaze fell to the aged envelope and letter on his desk. "You opened it."

"I didn't see that I had any choice."

"And...are you all right?"

"I'm working on it."

She stepped into the room. "That's a bit difficult to interpret."

He knew what she was asking and slid the letter across the desk. It shook in her hands, too, though considering what they'd been through in the past twenty-four hours, that came as no surprise. What moved him profoundly, however, was seeing the streaks of wetness that soon coursed down her cheeks. He should have known her tears would be as generous as a spring rain. She was the type of woman who would cry for everyone but herself.

"Congratulations," she murmured at last. "Dreams do come true."

"Some."

"Your mother was a special woman."

"I know. That's what made what happened to her all the more terrible. My God, she was already carrying me. She must have told him."

"Maybe. If she knew."

"Even if she guessed, she *would* have told the lousy—" Navarrone bit off the rest and shook his head.

"I think—" Erin's eyes glistened like twin pools of liquid emeralds "—he was obsessed with her, Navarrone."

"He made her life a shadow of what it should have been. He stole from both my parents."

"You're right, of course. What he did can never be excused. But last night we spoke briefly—before I made him angry and he threw me out. I had the opportunity to glimpse the torment he'd been living with all these years. He never stopped wanting her. I think he may even have proposed to her, before or afterward, I have no idea. It's just a hunch, something about the way he looked, what he said. When she rejected him, she was rejecting everything he was, everything he'd accomplished. He couldn't understand that, and he was never able to resolve it in his mind. Here he was offering her the world, and she chose to stay with a man who would always have far less of everything—except love."

"She didn't need more. My fa...my father," he said more slowly, the word calming him like a balm, "was her entire life."

"Part," Erin corrected gently, and set the letter back on his desk. "She says as much here. Your father taught her about true love, Navarrone. But *you* allowed her to share it. You were living proof that out of the worst tragedy can come good."

Navarrone eyed the letter and realized she was right. Still... "I don't think I'll be able to forgive him the way she did," he confessed.

"It took her years. Give yourself time. So much of you has been living in the past. Once you start to look toward the future, you might surprise yourself." When he remained silent after that, she rubbed her palms against her thighs in the nervous gesture he was beginning to recognize. "I was wondering what kind of reception I'd get once I got here."

Her weak attempt to sound conversational had Navarrone pushing himself to his feet and crossing toward her. "Come here and I'll show you," he replied, already reaching for her.

She came to him with a burst of energy that belied her obvious state of fatigue. Dared he hope she could forgive him his own huge mistakes? Dared he believe she needed him as much as he needed her? There was, he realized, a price to pay for letting go of the past, in this case a humbling one. It left him with a vast emptiness, no less deep than the caverns their state was famous for.

He buried his face against her hair and filled himself with her scent. "What I said to you before . . ."

"I know you didn't mean it."

"Unfortunately I did." When she leaned back and stared wide-eyed, he couldn't resist stroking away a lingering teardrop from her lower eyelashes with his thumb. "I was sick with jealousy, Slim. Even now that I know Griff's not my half brother."

"If I'd felt anything but friendship for him, do you think I would have joined the Peace Corps or accepted Paul's proposal?"

He gave a rueful shake of his head. "All I could see was that you always came to his defense."

"I was defending a memory," she corrected, shame reverberating in her voice as much as sadness. She laid her head against his shoulder. "I didn't recognize the man we faced today, Navarrone. I still can't believe he could be so cruel."

"I was wrong, too. I thought it was Caulfield and maybe a few others operating under Marsh's orders. I didn't think Griff had the stomach. Talk about misreading a person."

"Before they took him away, I asked him about last night. I needed to understand how he could leave a party to do what he did. He told me the party made it all the more perfect, that he'd known about the horses grouping there and that all the company would provide him with innumerable witnesses. He just hadn't counted on my leaving early."

"I'm sorry," Navarrone murmured, kissing her forehead. "This is hitting you hard, too, but maybe in time you'll see, as I'm beginning to, that it was building up for years. He never had a chance, living in Marsh's shadow the way he did. People like Marsh suffocate the life out of weaker individuals."

"You underestimate what your own effect was on him. He saw you as the son Marsh aspired to have. Strong, independent, purposeful. Griff saw that every time you and Marsh butted heads, and it slowly ate away at him like a cancer."

"Well, it's over," Navarrone said decisively. "At least he's finished around here."

"Sounds like things may get kind of quiet in these parts," Erin said, taking a deep breath and glancing up at him. "Whatever will you do for excitement, Chief Santee?"

"Before or after I make love with you?" he murmured, a smile tugging at his mouth.

She stroked her finger along his mustache. "This is the way it should have been for us. You teased and flirted with me from the first, remember?" Her gaze turned wistful. "We haven't had much cause to be lighthearted since."

"No, but I have a feeling we can handle anything after this. I'm in love with you, Slim. Have you figured that out yet?"

The joy that quickly spread across her fatigue-shadowed face created an image of fragile beauty. It was a moment Navarrone knew he would carry to his grave. But it lasted only a second. In the next she was kissing him, and all he could concentrate on was how to absorb everything she had to give.

He stroked his hands up and down her back, slid them into her hair. He met the ladylike yet eager parry of her tongue with masculine demand, and felt his body catch fire under the subtle assault of her lithe body. Only hours ago they'd sated themselves in each other's arms, but it might as well have been days.

When he raised his head, he was all seriousness. "I need the words, Slim."

"I love you, Navarrone."

Relief and pleasure carried the punch of twelve-year-old Scotch on an empty stomach. He took hold of her hand and pressed a kiss to her palm. "Enough to take the risk of marrying me, even though we've barely known each other more than a month?"

Erin tilted her head and eyed him mischievously. "I rather like the idea of spending the next fifty or seventy-five years discovering who my husband is."

"It may take a while to say goodbye to all our ghosts."

"I'll love away your ghosts, the way you've been loving away mine," she murmured, touching her mouth to his. "I'll make you laugh when you're sad. I'll listen when you need to talk, and I'll try not to get too hung up in the gray areas when you want my opinion about something. I'll be

your friend, your lover, the missing half of your soul—and
you'll be mine.''

Navarrone crushed her to him, praying they would have
enough years for him to do and be all that for her, and more.

Epilogue

He remained still and silent until she'd tiptoed across th
room and set her shoes by the closet door.

"I'm not asleep."

Erin went to the bathroom and turned on the light, the
shutting the door halfway, came to the bed and into hi
arms. "Hi," she murmured, giving him one of those warm
tender kisses he'd grown addicted to in their eight month
of marriage. "Miss me?"

"Why do you think I was snoozing with one eye open'
How'd it go?"

"They had a boy. A little tank, all of nine pounds, tw
ounces."

Navarrone winced in sympathy. "Is the mother all right?'

"Exhausted, but very proud of herself."

"I'll bet. Their excellent doctor should be proud of her
self, too," he murmured, helping her as she began peeling
off her clothes.

"*She's* beat. I feel as though every muscle in my body has a knot."

Navarrone reached up to take the pins out of her hair with an expertise derived from devout practice. The faster he could get her comfortable, the sooner she would be in bed with him, as he yearned for her to be. "Sounds as though you could use a thorough massage."

"Oh, sweetheart, I can't ask you for that. You need your rest for that trip to Albuquerque tomorrow."

"So do you."

"But I can always catch a nap on the drive up."

Van Caulfield's trial was scheduled to start tomorrow. Both Navarrone and Erin had been called as witnesses for the prosecution. Only last week they'd learned that, though the Keegan attorneys had succeeded in getting a change of venue, moving both Van's and Griff's trials up to the city, their attorneys had run out of continuances. Griff's trial was scheduled to begin the first week in May. By then the new owners of the Silver Edge would have taken over the ranch.

As he tossed back the bed sheet and coaxed his wife to lie on her stomach, Navarrone once again felt the absolute pride and passion of loving this special woman. As they had tonight, their jobs occasionally challenged their ability to be together as much as they might like—especially since her practice was doing so well and the little filly they'd taken in had coaxed him into getting back into raising and training horses in his free time—but they made the most of every minute they had.

Now, as he sat on his heels to begin massaging her tense shoulder and back muscles, he knew that he'd only understood the outer perimeters of what loving really meant that day he and Erin had exchanged their vows, only weeks after the episode at the Silver Edge. Every day she taught him a new lesson, and every night, as she drifted off to sleep in his arms, he found another reason to give thanks for the miracle that had brought her to him.

"Oh, that feels heavenly," Erin sighed, her throaty voice getting to him as it always did. "By the way, Gramps said he and Teresa will keep the clinic open tomorrow in case there's any walk-ins."

"Best thing you ever did for him was let him participate more so he feels he still has a purpose."

"I'm the one who's benefiting the most. I couldn't get through the day without his and Teresa's help."

Hearing the resurgence of fatigue in her voice gave Navarrone an idea. "We're supposed to be among the first witnesses called, so afterward, why don't we plan to have lunch somewhere quiet and romantic?"

"I can get through anything knowing I have that to look forward to."

Navarrone bent to place two light kisses on either dimple at the small of her back. "If you get nervous while up on the stand, just look at me and know I'll be loving you no matter what you feel you have to say."

Erin rolled onto her back and drew him down to her. "I love you so much," she whispered, offering him her mouth.

Hungrily he kissed her, and desire rose swiftly, as it always did between them. Using his fingers to coax her nipples into hard little peaks, Navarrone shifted to settle himself closer to the source of her heat. "I know what would really relax you."

"You."

"Inside you."

"Hot and hard."

"And massaging away that tension from the inside out."

Sighing with deep content, Erin murmured, "You always know exactly how to fire my imagination."

"Speaking of imagination, what do you think our chances are of getting you a little nine-pound-two-ounce tank?" She'd stayed on the Pill for two months after they were married. To give themselves time to get over the hectic events of their lives, they'd decided, as well as to simply enjoy each other. But every day he shared with Erin, Navarrone knew he wanted it all—and that included having a family.

"The odds aren't very good with so much distance between us."

He smiled, but the smile soon turned to a groan as she took him in her slender, gifted hand and guided him to where he most wanted to be. Every inch of him came alive, and he buried himself deep, worshiping the feel of her. As was often the case, their loving was fast and feverish, neither of them yet able to believe that they had found such happiness. Besides which, Navarrone thought, burying his hands in her silky hair, Erin had a tendency to go straight to his head, and this time was proving no different.

"Oh, damn..." he ground out.

"What?"

"Don't lick me there."

"You don't like it?"

"I love it."

"So what's the...problem?"

"That."

"Ah...but that's good."

"Baby, that's—" he couldn't finish because it was already happening and he liked to kiss her at that moment, absorb the seductive sounds she made, just as she absorbed him into her sweet body "—perfect," he finally mouthed against her lips.

When she thought he'd fallen asleep, Erin eased out from under the protective arm wrapped around her and tiptoed to the bathroom. There she slipped on the short terry-cloth wrap she kept on the back of the door and went to the kitchen where she poured herself a glass of milk. Loving made her thirsty, and these days, more than ever, she wanted to make sure she got all her nutrients.

Glass in hand, she picked up the photo that continued to have its special place on the lunch bar, and walked over to the window. A nearly full moon was high in the sky, casting the earth in a silver mantle of mystery and beauty. It also made the woman and man looking back at her from the photo seem particularly close tonight. After taking another sip of her milk, Erin sighed and, holding the photo against her chest, looked up at the stars twinkling in a sea of indigo.

"Anna," she whispered to the woman with whom she felt a strange close bond. "You and James are going to be grandparents."

From behind her came the sound of footsteps. "Slim?" Navarrone put his arms around her and drew her back against his powerful, naked body. "What's wrong, baby?"

"Not a thing," she replied, putting down the photo and turning to face him. She should have known he would miss her. Neither of them slept well when they weren't together. "I was thirsty and I wanted some milk."

"Milk? Since when have you started liking milk?"

Placing a kiss where his heart beat strongly, Erin took his hand and drew him toward the bedroom. "Come to bed, darling. There's something I want to tell you."

* * * * *

SILHOUETTE® Desire™
MAN OF THE MONTH

**YOU'VE ASKED FOR IT,
YOU'VE GOT IT!
MAN OF THE MONTH: 1992**

ONLY FROM SILHOUETTE DESIRE

You just couldn't get enough of them, those men from Silhouette Desire—twelve sinfully sexy, delightfully devilish heroes. Some will make you sweat, some will make you sigh . . . but every long, lean one of them will have you swooning. So here they are, *more* of the men we couldn't resist bringing to you for one more year. . . .

BEST MAN FOR THE JOB
by Dixie Browning in June

MIDNIGHT RIDER
by Cait London in July

CONVENIENT HUSBAND
by Joan Hohl in August

NAVARRONE
by Helen R. Myers in September

A MAN OF HONOR
by Paula Detmer Riggs in October

BLUE SKY GUY
by Carole Buck in November

IT HAD TO BE YOU
by Jennifer Greene in December

Don't let these men get away! MAN OF THE MONTH, only in Silhouette Desire!

MOM92JD

Take 4 bestselling love stories FREE

Plus get a FREE surprise gift!

Special Limited-time Offer

Mail to Silhouette Reader Service™

In the U.S.	In Canada
3010 Walden Avenue	P.O. Box 609
P.O. Box 1867	Fort Erie, Ontario
Buffalo, N.Y. 14269-1867	L2A 5X3

YES! Please send me 4 free Silhouette Desire® novels and my free surprise gift. Then send me 6 brand-new novels every month, which I will receive months before they appear in bookstores. Bill me at the low price of $2.49* each—a savings of 40¢ apiece off the cover prices. There are no shipping, handling or other hidden costs. I understand that accepting the books and gift places me under no obligation ever to buy any books. I can always return a shipment and cancel at any time. Even if I never buy another book from Silhouette, the 4 free books and the surprise gift are mine to keep forever.

*Offer slightly different in Canada—$2.49 per book plus 69¢ per shipment for delivery. Canadian residents add applicable federal and provincial sales tax. Sales tax applicable in N.Y.

225 BPA ADMA   326 BPA ADMP

Name _____ (PLEASE PRINT)

Address _____ Apt. No. _____

City _____ State/Prov. _____ Zip/Postal Code. _____

This offer is limited to one order per household and not valid to present Silhouette Desire® subscribers. Terms and prices are subject to change.

DES-92   © 1990 Harlequin Enterprises Limited

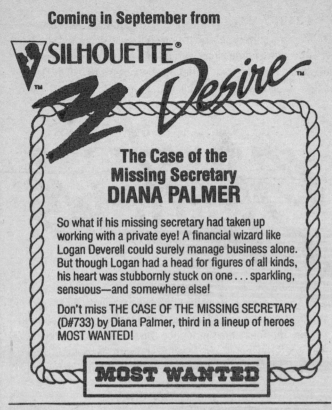

TAKE A WALK ON THE DARK SIDE OF LOVE

October is the shivery season, when chill winds blow and shadows walk the night. Come along with us into a haunting world where love and danger go hand in hand, where passions will thrill you and dangers will chill you. Come with us to

In this newest short story collection from Silhouette Books, three of your favorite authors tell tales just perfect for a spooky autumn night. Let Anne Stuart introduce you to "The Monster in the Closet," Helen R. Myers bewitch you with "Seawitch," and Heather Graham Pozzessere entice you with "Wilde Imaginings."

Silhouette Shadows™
Haunting a store near you this October.

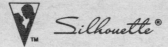